POWER PLAY

A GRAPHIC GUIDE ADVENTURE

WITHDRAWN

WRITTEN BY
LIAM O'DONNELL

ILLUSTRATED BY
MIKE DEAS

ORCA BOOK PUBLISHERS

For Melanie, my wife. Thanks to Marie for her advice with this one and much more. —LOD

Text copyright © 2011 Liam O'Donnell
Illustrations copyright © 2011 Mike Deas

Library and Archives Canada Cataloguing in Publication

O'Donnell, Liam, 1970-
Power play : a graphic guide adventure / written by Liam O'Donnell ;
illustrated by Mike Deas.

Issued also in electronic format.
ISBN 978-1-55469-069-5

1. World politics--Comic books, strips, etc.--Juvenile fiction.
2. Graphic novels. I. Deas, Mike, 1982- . II. Title.
PS8579 D647.P69 2011   J741.5f971   C2010-907886-1

First published in the United States, 2011
Library of Congress Control Number: 2010941867

Summary: It's a fight against the planet's power players as the kids dive into the world of politics, uncovering how
government works, the history of democracy, the influence of lobbyists and corporations on politicians
and the potential of civil society to change it all.

Disclaimer: This book is a work of fiction and is intended for entertainment purposes only. The author
and/or publisher accepts no responsibility for misuse or misinterpretation of the information in this book.

Orca Book Publishers gratefully acknowledges the support for its publishing programs provided
by the following agencies: the Government of Canada through the Canada Book Fund and the
Canada Council for the Arts, and the Province of British Columbia through the BC Arts Council
and the Book Publishing Tax Credit.

Cover and interior artwork by Mike Deas
Cover layout by Teresa Bubela
Author photo by Melanie McBride • Illustrator photo by Ellen Ho

ORCA BOOK PUBLISHERS   ORCA BOOK PUBLISHERS
PO Box 5626, Stn. B   PO Box 468
Victoria, BC Canada   Custer, WA USA
V8R 6S4   98240-0468

www.orcabook.com
Printed and bound in Hong Kong.

14 13 12 11 • 4 3 2 1

CHAPTER I

NOT-SO-WARM WELCOME

EVER WONDER WHO IS IN CHARGE? I DON'T MEAN JUST AT SCHOOL OR AT HOME. I'M TALKING WHO IS IN CHARGE OF EVERYTHING.

WHO DECIDED WE HAVE TO WEAR SEAT BELTS IN A CAR? WHO MADE THE LAWS THAT SAY YOU CAN'T JUST TAKE SOMEBODY'S STUFF? DEEP QUESTIONS, I KNOW.

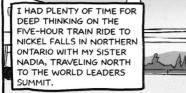

I HAD PLENTY OF TIME FOR DEEP THINKING ON THE FIVE-HOUR TRAIN RIDE TO NICKEL FALLS IN NORTHERN ONTARIO WITH MY SISTER NADIA, TRAVELING NORTH TO THE WORLD LEADERS SUMMIT.

POLITICIANS FROM AROUND THE WORLD ARE POURING INTO NICKEL FALLS TO TALK ABOUT THE LAWS WE ALL LIVE BY AND TO MAKE NEW ONES.

WE'VE SWAPPED TRAINS FOR PLANES AND COME TO THE AIRPORT TO MEET AN OLD FRIEND.

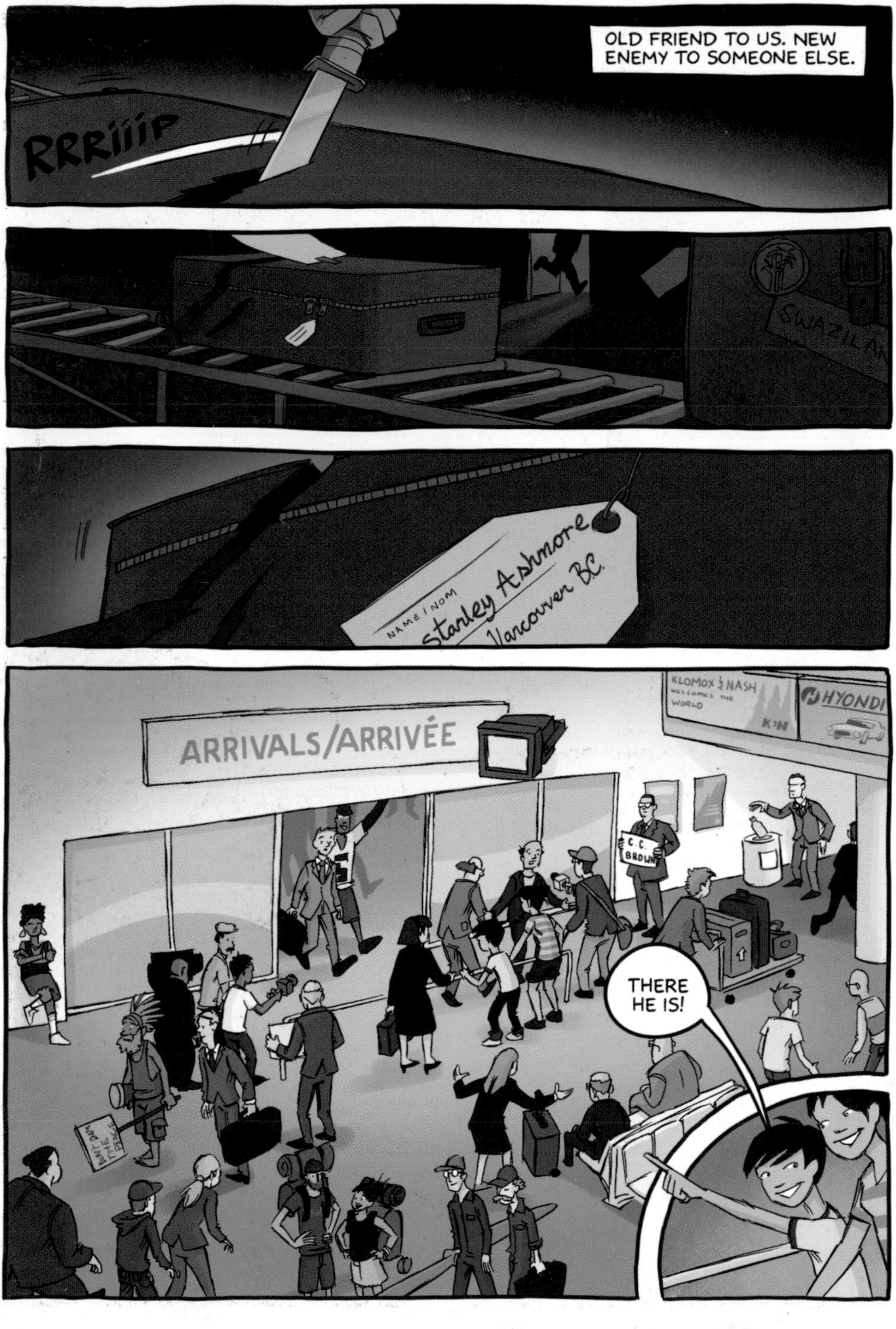
OLD FRIEND TO US. NEW ENEMY TO SOMEONE ELSE.
RRRiiiP
SWAZILAN
NAME | NOM
Stanley Ashmore
Vancouver B.C.
ARRIVALS/ARRIVÉE
KLOMOX & NASH
WELCOMES THE WORLD
HYONDI
C.C. BROWN
DON'T DAM THE PEACE
THERE HE IS!

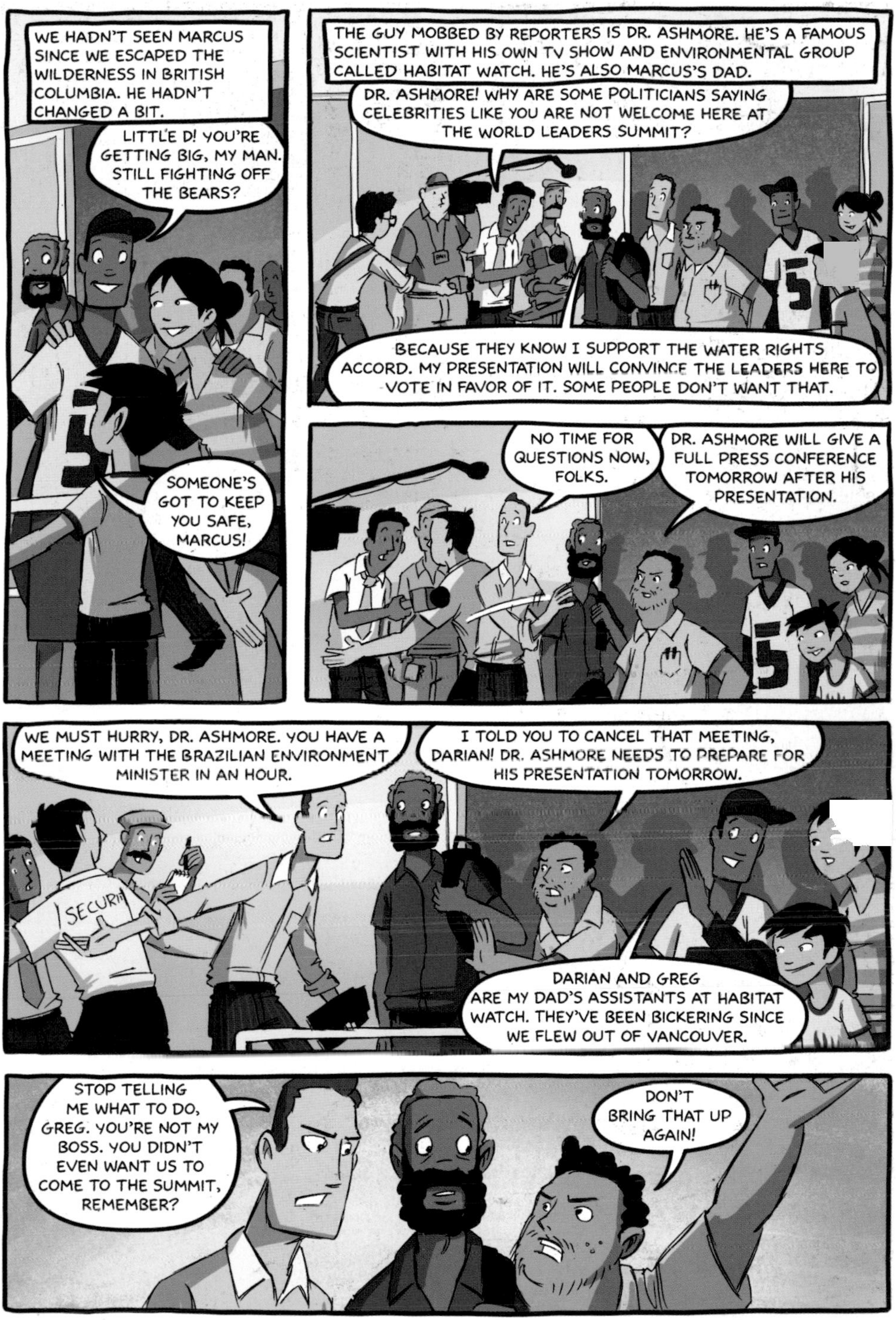

WE HADN'T SEEN MARCUS SINCE WE ESCAPED THE WILDERNESS IN BRITISH COLUMBIA. HE HADN'T CHANGED A BIT.
LITTLE D! YOU'RE GETTING BIG, MY MAN. STILL FIGHTING OFF THE BEARS?
SOMEONE'S GOT TO KEEP YOU SAFE, MARCUS!
THE GUY MOBBED BY REPORTERS IS DR. ASHMORE. HE'S A FAMOUS SCIENTIST WITH HIS OWN TV SHOW AND ENVIRONMENTAL GROUP CALLED HABITAT WATCH. HE'S ALSO MARCUS'S DAD.
DR. ASHMORE! WHY ARE SOME POLITICIANS SAYING CELEBRITIES LIKE YOU ARE NOT WELCOME HERE AT THE WORLD LEADERS SUMMIT?
BECAUSE THEY KNOW I SUPPORT THE WATER RIGHTS ACCORD. MY PRESENTATION WILL CONVINCE THE LEADERS HERE TO VOTE IN FAVOR OF IT. SOME PEOPLE DON'T WANT THAT.
NO TIME FOR QUESTIONS NOW, FOLKS.
DR. ASHMORE WILL GIVE A FULL PRESS CONFERENCE TOMORROW AFTER HIS PRESENTATION.
WE MUST HURRY, DR. ASHMORE. YOU HAVE A MEETING WITH THE BRAZILIAN ENVIRONMENT MINISTER IN AN HOUR.
I TOLD YOU TO CANCEL THAT MEETING, DARIAN! DR. ASHMORE NEEDS TO PREPARE FOR HIS PRESENTATION TOMORROW.
SECURI
DARIAN AND GREG ARE MY DAD'S ASSISTANTS AT HABITAT WATCH. THEY'VE BEEN BICKERING SINCE WE FLEW OUT OF VANCOUVER.
STOP TELLING ME WHAT TO DO, GREG. YOU'RE NOT MY BOSS. YOU DIDN'T EVEN WANT US TO COME TO THE SUMMIT, REMEMBER?
DON'T BRING THAT UP AGAIN!

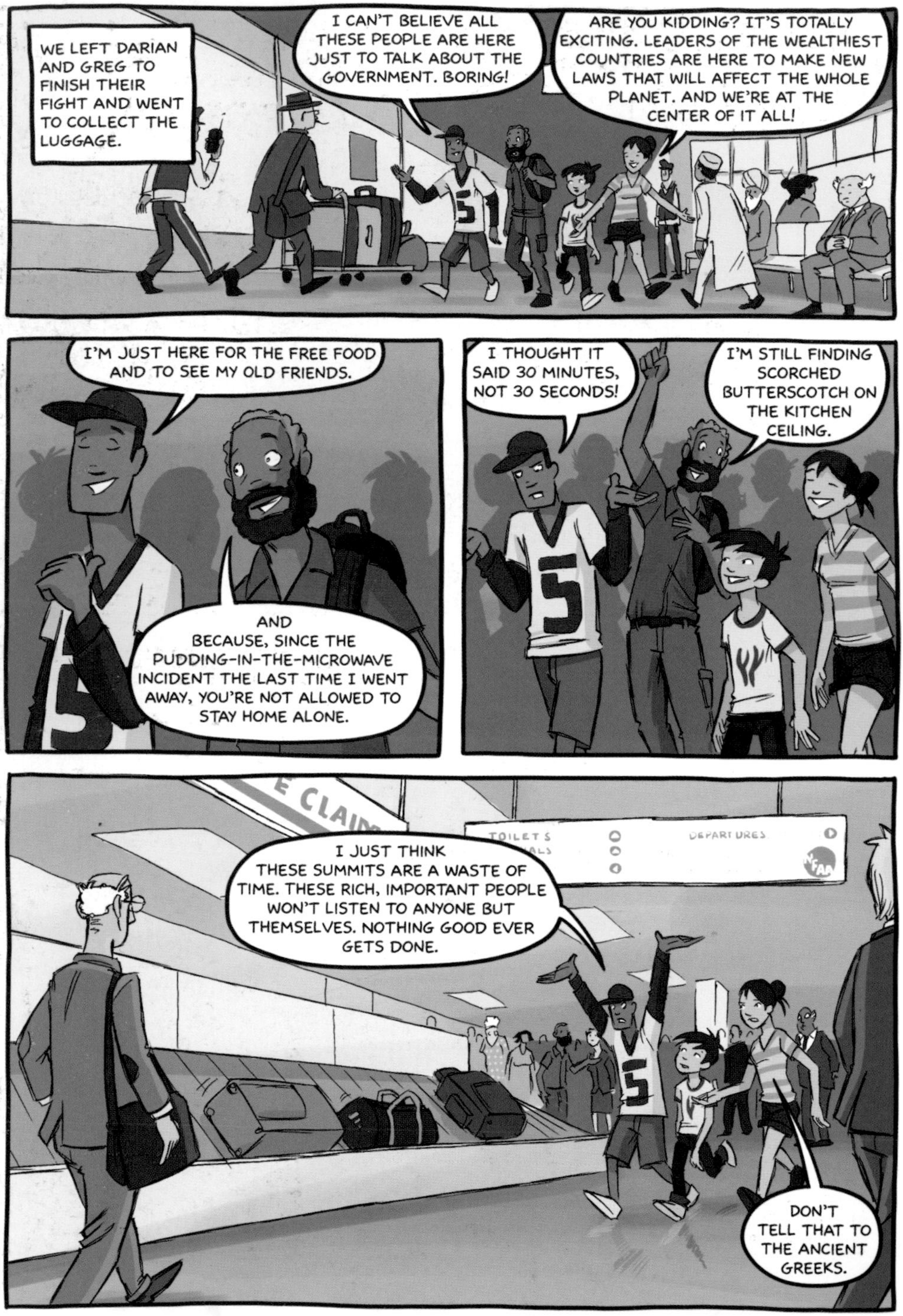
WE LEFT DARIAN AND GREG TO FINISH THEIR FIGHT AND WENT TO COLLECT THE LUGGAGE.
I CAN'T BELIEVE ALL THESE PEOPLE ARE HERE JUST TO TALK ABOUT THE GOVERNMENT. BORING!
ARE YOU KIDDING? IT'S TOTALLY EXCITING. LEADERS OF THE WEALTHIEST COUNTRIES ARE HERE TO MAKE NEW LAWS THAT WILL AFFECT THE WHOLE PLANET. AND WE'RE AT THE CENTER OF IT ALL!
I'M JUST HERE FOR THE FREE FOOD AND TO SEE MY OLD FRIENDS.
AND BECAUSE, SINCE THE PUDDING-IN-THE-MICROWAVE INCIDENT THE LAST TIME I WENT AWAY, YOU'RE NOT ALLOWED TO STAY HOME ALONE.
I THOUGHT IT SAID 30 MINUTES, NOT 30 SECONDS!
I'M STILL FINDING SCORCHED BUTTERSCOTCH ON THE KITCHEN CEILING.
TOILETS
DEPARTURES
I JUST THINK THESE SUMMITS ARE A WASTE OF TIME. THESE RICH, IMPORTANT PEOPLE WON'T LISTEN TO ANYONE BUT THEMSELVES. NOTHING GOOD EVER GETS DONE.
DON'T TELL THAT TO THE ANCIENT GREEKS.

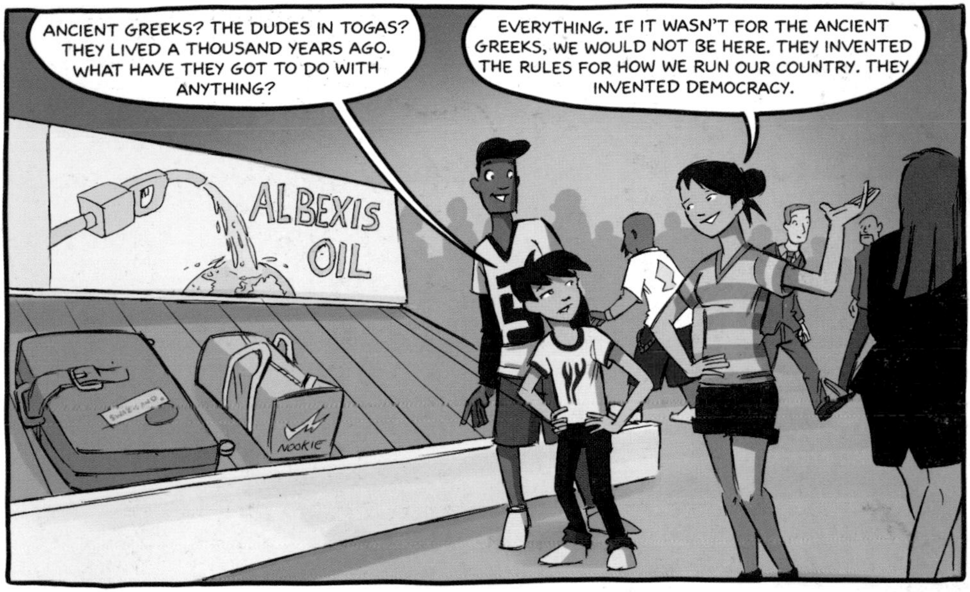
ANCIENT GREEKS? THE DUDES IN TOGAS? THEY LIVED A THOUSAND YEARS AGO. WHAT HAVE THEY GOT TO DO WITH ANYTHING?
EVERYTHING. IF IT WASN'T FOR THE ANCIENT GREEKS, WE WOULD NOT BE HERE. THEY INVENTED THE RULES FOR HOW WE RUN OUR COUNTRY. THEY INVENTED DEMOCRACY.
ALBEXIS OIL
NOOKIE

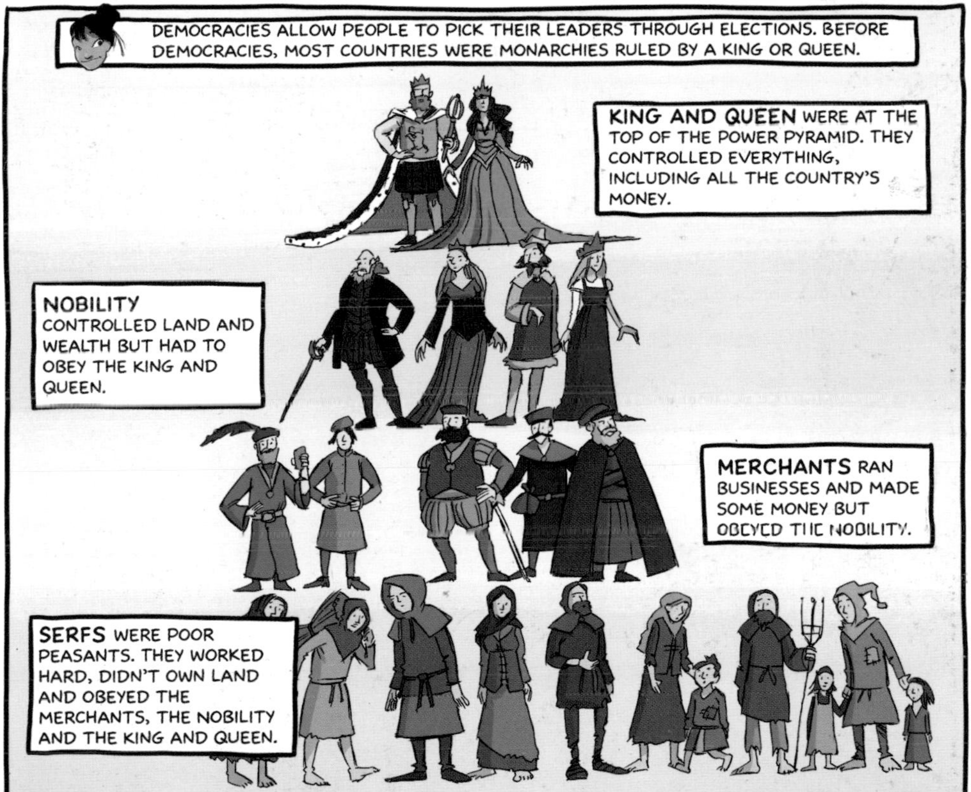
DEMOCRACIES ALLOW PEOPLE TO PICK THEIR LEADERS THROUGH ELECTIONS. BEFORE DEMOCRACIES, MOST COUNTRIES WERE MONARCHIES RULED BY A KING OR QUEEN.
KING AND QUEEN WERE AT THE TOP OF THE POWER PYRAMID. THEY CONTROLLED EVERYTHING, INCLUDING ALL THE COUNTRY'S MONEY.
NOBILITY CONTROLLED LAND AND WEALTH BUT HAD TO OBEY THE KING AND QUEEN.
MERCHANTS RAN BUSINESSES AND MADE SOME MONEY BUT OBEYED THE NOBILITY.
SERFS WERE POOR PEASANTS. THEY WORKED HARD, DIDN'T OWN LAND AND OBEYED THE MERCHANTS, THE NOBILITY AND THE KING AND QUEEN.

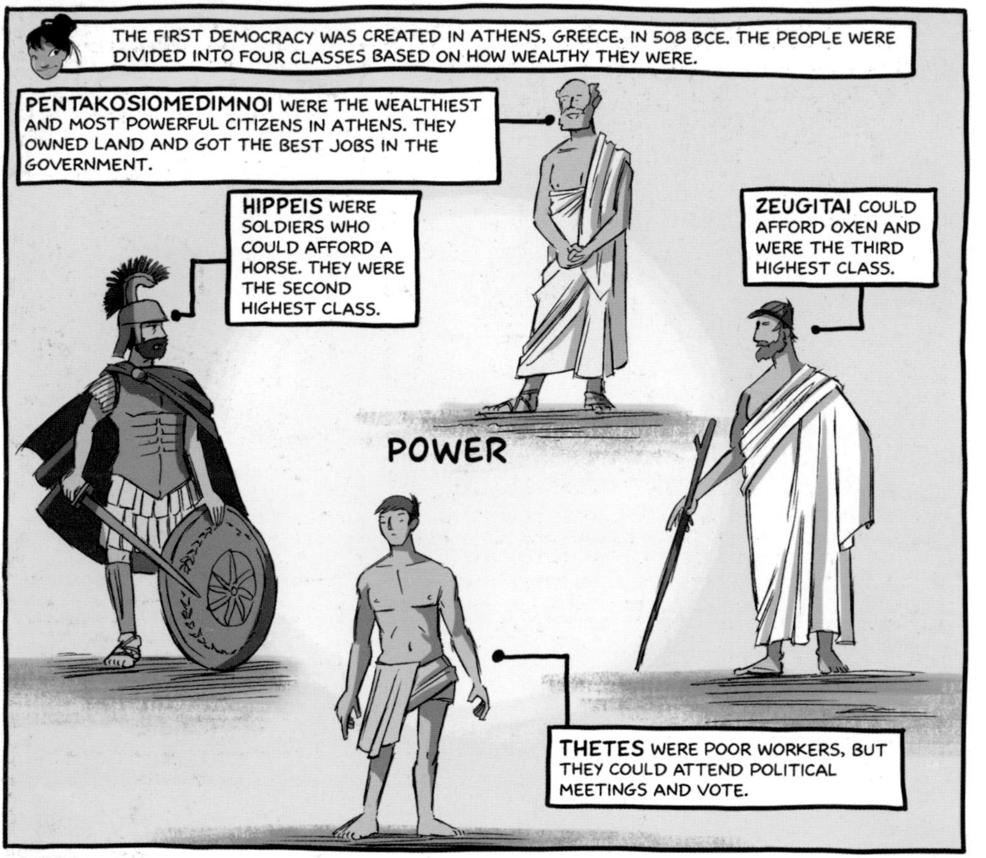
THE FIRST DEMOCRACY WAS CREATED IN ATHENS, GREECE, IN 508 BCE. THE PEOPLE WERE DIVIDED INTO FOUR CLASSES BASED ON HOW WEALTHY THEY WERE.
PENTAKOSIOMEDIMNOI WERE THE WEALTHIEST AND MOST POWERFUL CITIZENS IN ATHENS. THEY OWNED LAND AND GOT THE BEST JOBS IN THE GOVERNMENT.
HIPPEIS WERE SOLDIERS WHO COULD AFFORD A HORSE. THEY WERE THE SECOND HIGHEST CLASS.
ZEUGITAI COULD AFFORD OXEN AND WERE THE THIRD HIGHEST CLASS.
POWER
THETES WERE POOR WORKERS, BUT THEY COULD ATTEND POLITICAL MEETINGS AND VOTE.

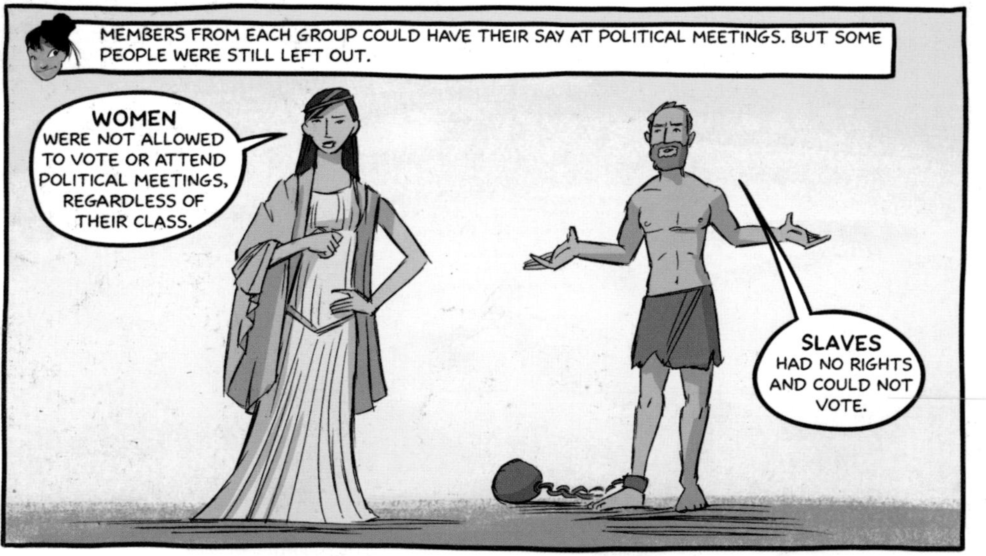
MEMBERS FROM EACH GROUP COULD HAVE THEIR SAY AT POLITICAL MEETINGS. BUT SOME PEOPLE WERE STILL LEFT OUT.
WOMEN WERE NOT ALLOWED TO VOTE OR ATTEND POLITICAL MEETINGS, REGARDLESS OF THEIR CLASS.
SLAVES HAD NO RIGHTS AND COULD NOT VOTE.

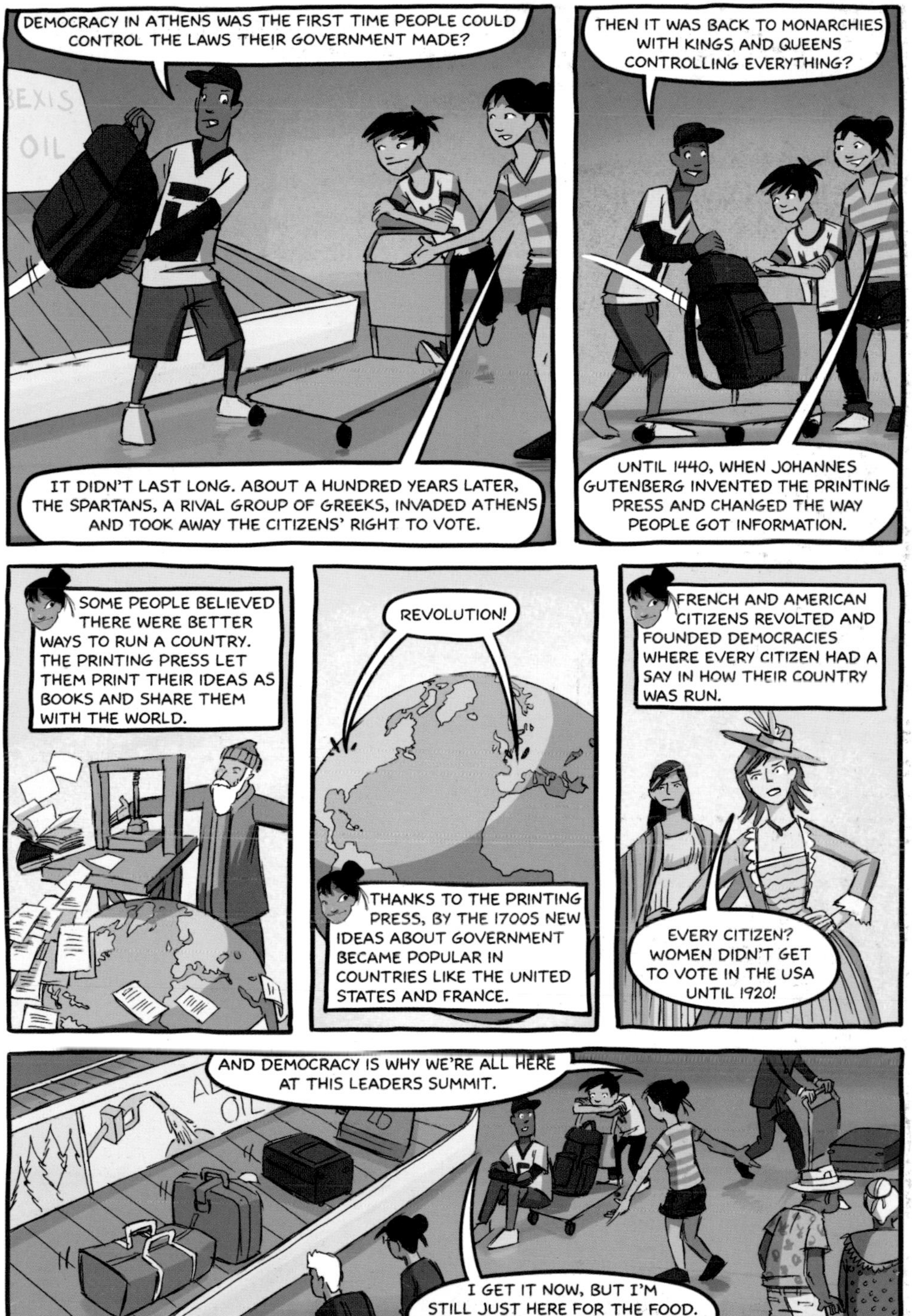

DEMOCRACY IN ATHENS WAS THE FIRST TIME PEOPLE COULD CONTROL THE LAWS THEIR GOVERNMENT MADE?
BEXIS OIL
IT DIDN'T LAST LONG. ABOUT A HUNDRED YEARS LATER, THE SPARTANS, A RIVAL GROUP OF GREEKS, INVADED ATHENS AND TOOK AWAY THE CITIZENS' RIGHT TO VOTE.
THEN IT WAS BACK TO MONARCHIES WITH KINGS AND QUEENS CONTROLLING EVERYTHING?
UNTIL 1440, WHEN JOHANNES GUTENBERG INVENTED THE PRINTING PRESS AND CHANGED THE WAY PEOPLE GOT INFORMATION.
SOME PEOPLE BELIEVED THERE WERE BETTER WAYS TO RUN A COUNTRY. THE PRINTING PRESS LET THEM PRINT THEIR IDEAS AS BOOKS AND SHARE THEM WITH THE WORLD.
REVOLUTION!
THANKS TO THE PRINTING PRESS, BY THE 1700S NEW IDEAS ABOUT GOVERNMENT BECAME POPULAR IN COUNTRIES LIKE THE UNITED STATES AND FRANCE.
FRENCH AND AMERICAN CITIZENS REVOLTED AND FOUNDED DEMOCRACIES WHERE EVERY CITIZEN HAD A SAY IN HOW THEIR COUNTRY WAS RUN.
EVERY CITIZEN? WOMEN DIDN'T GET TO VOTE IN THE USA UNTIL 1920!
AND DEMOCRACY IS WHY WE'RE ALL HERE AT THIS LEADERS SUMMIT.
I GET IT NOW, BUT I'M STILL JUST HERE FOR THE FOOD.

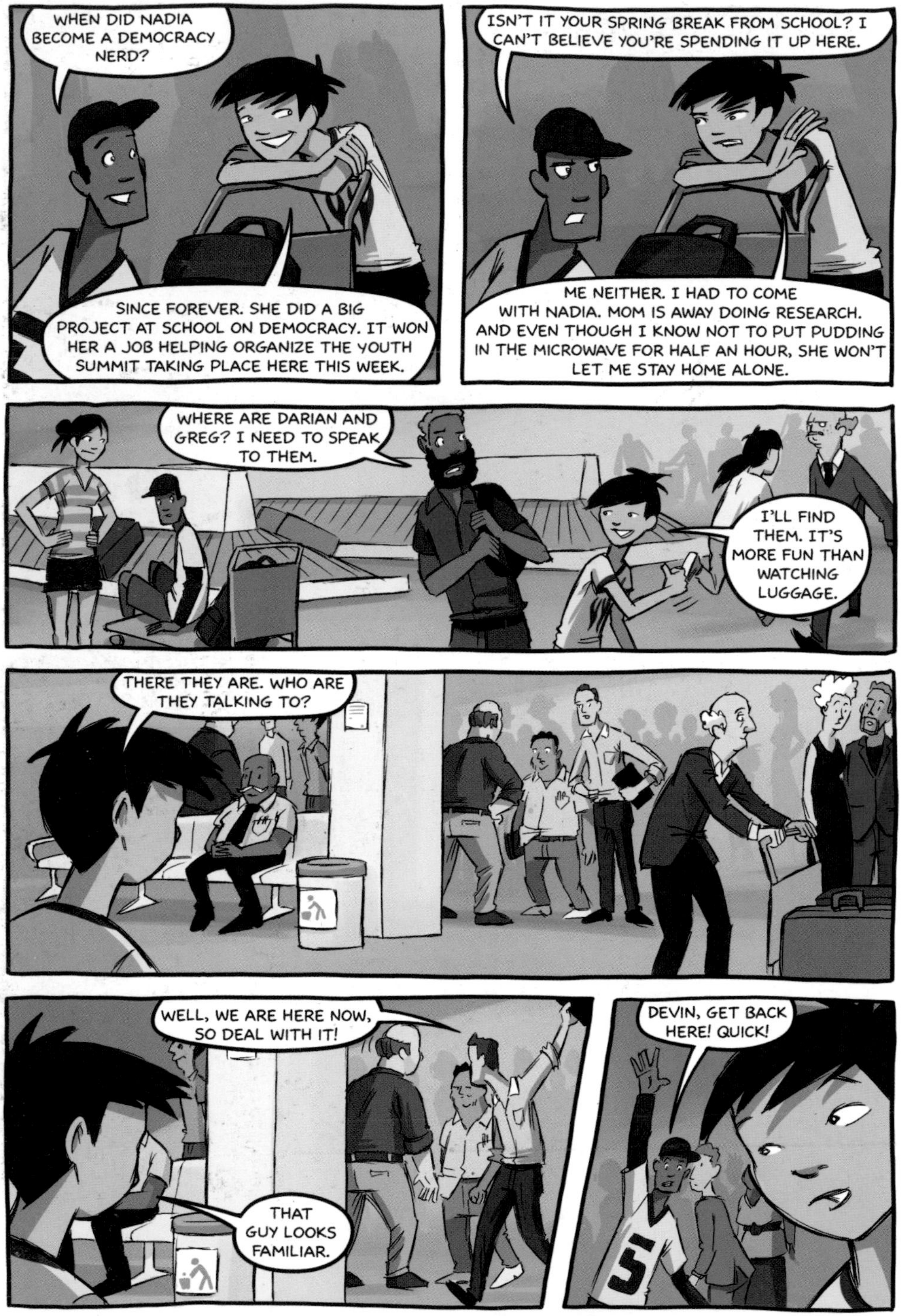
WHEN DID NADIA BECOME A DEMOCRACY NERD?
SINCE FOREVER. SHE DID A BIG PROJECT AT SCHOOL ON DEMOCRACY. IT WON HER A JOB HELPING ORGANIZE THE YOUTH SUMMIT TAKING PLACE HERE THIS WEEK.
ISN'T IT YOUR SPRING BREAK FROM SCHOOL? I CAN'T BELIEVE YOU'RE SPENDING IT UP HERE.
ME NEITHER. I HAD TO COME WITH NADIA. MOM IS AWAY DOING RESEARCH. AND EVEN THOUGH I KNOW NOT TO PUT PUDDING IN THE MICROWAVE FOR HALF AN HOUR, SHE WON'T LET ME STAY HOME ALONE.
WHERE ARE DARIAN AND GREG? I NEED TO SPEAK TO THEM.
I'LL FIND THEM. IT'S MORE FUN THAN WATCHING LUGGAGE.
THERE THEY ARE. WHO ARE THEY TALKING TO?
WELL, WE ARE HERE NOW, SO DEAL WITH IT!
THAT GUY LOOKS FAMILIAR.
DEVIN, GET BACK HERE! QUICK!

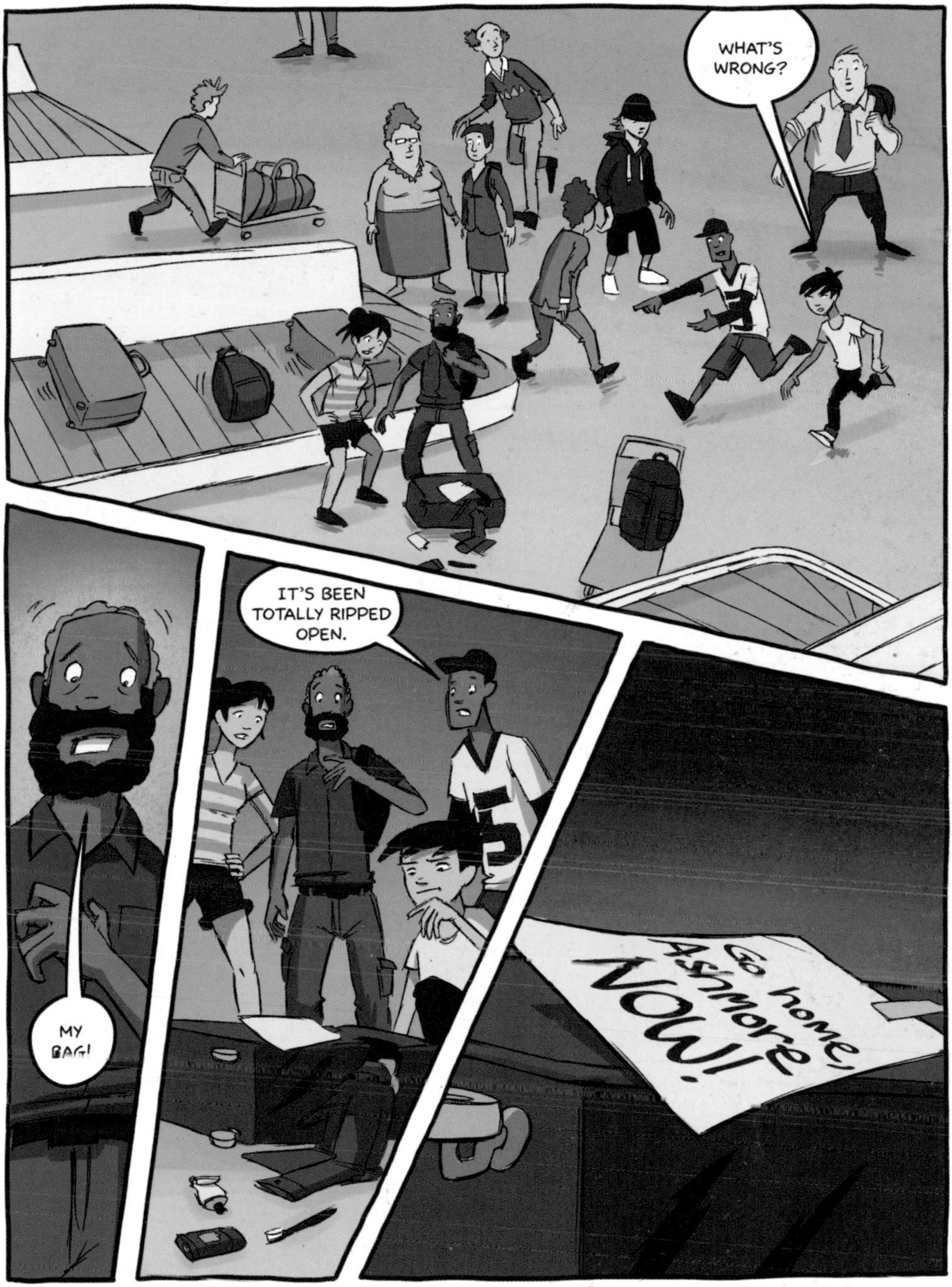
WHAT'S WRONG?
MY BAG!
IT'S BEEN TOTALLY RIPPED OPEN.
Go home, Ashmore, NOW!

CHAPTER 2
PUSHED TOO FAR

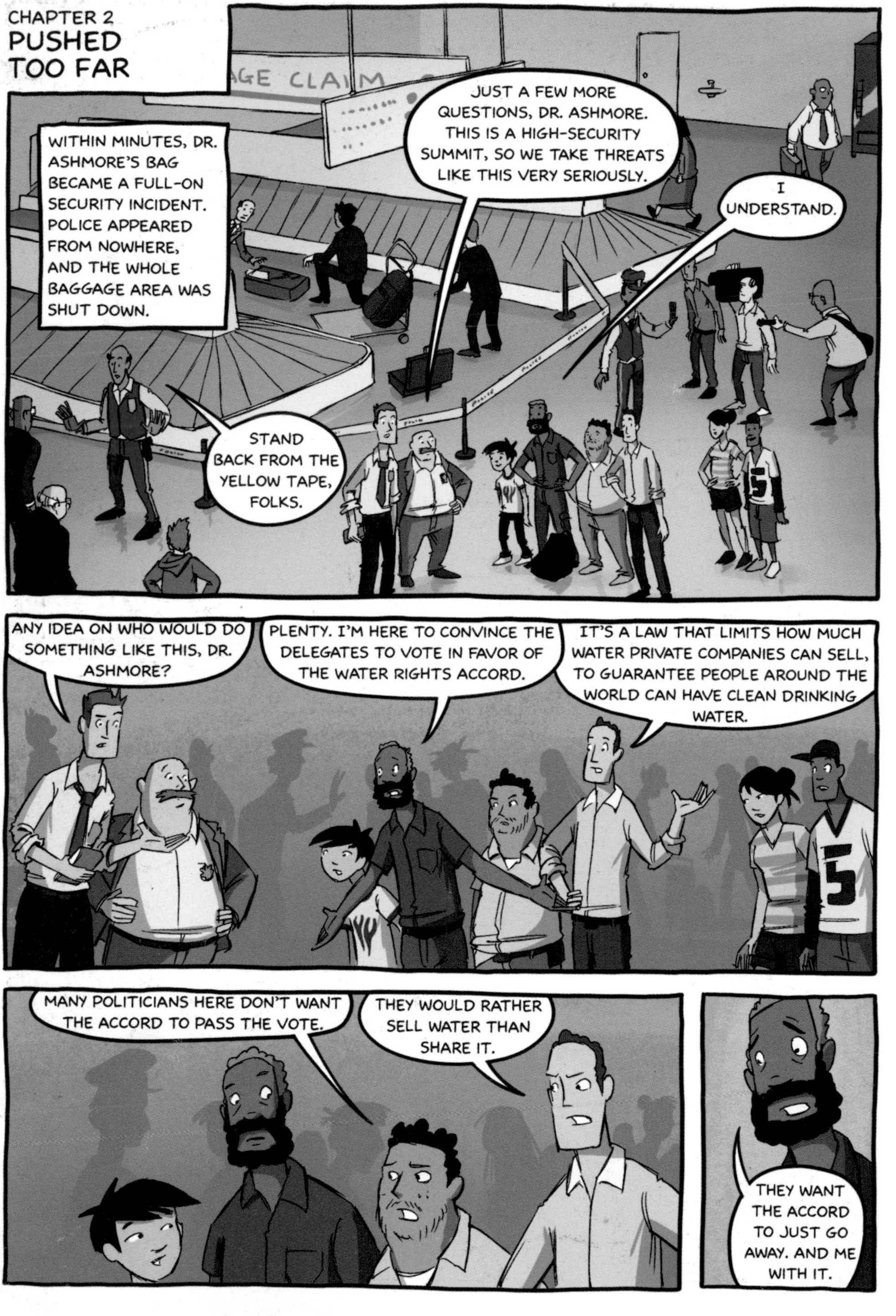

AGE CLAIM
WITHIN MINUTES, DR. ASHMORE'S BAG BECAME A FULL-ON SECURITY INCIDENT. POLICE APPEARED FROM NOWHERE, AND THE WHOLE BAGGAGE AREA WAS SHUT DOWN.
JUST A FEW MORE QUESTIONS, DR. ASHMORE. THIS IS A HIGH-SECURITY SUMMIT, SO WE TAKE THREATS LIKE THIS VERY SERIOUSLY.
I UNDERSTAND.
STAND BACK FROM THE YELLOW TAPE, FOLKS.
ANY IDEA ON WHO WOULD DO SOMETHING LIKE THIS, DR. ASHMORE?
PLENTY. I'M HERE TO CONVINCE THE DELEGATES TO VOTE IN FAVOR OF THE WATER RIGHTS ACCORD.
IT'S A LAW THAT LIMITS HOW MUCH WATER PRIVATE COMPANIES CAN SELL, TO GUARANTEE PEOPLE AROUND THE WORLD CAN HAVE CLEAN DRINKING WATER.
MANY POLITICIANS HERE DON'T WANT THE ACCORD TO PASS THE VOTE.
THEY WOULD RATHER SELL WATER THAN SHARE IT.
THEY WANT THE ACCORD TO JUST GO AWAY. AND ME WITH IT.

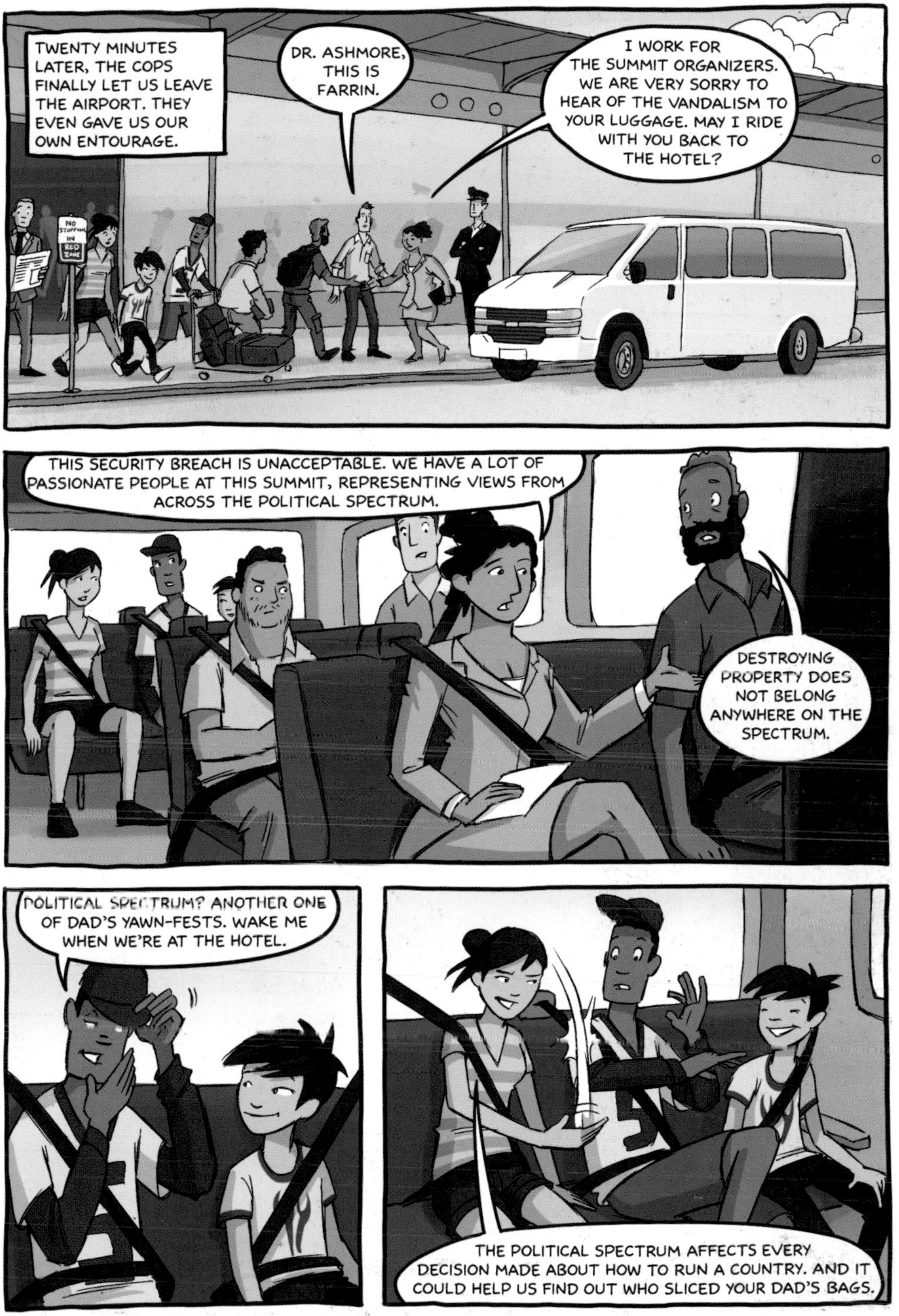
TWENTY MINUTES LATER, THE COPS FINALLY LET US LEAVE THE AIRPORT. THEY EVEN GAVE US OUR OWN ENTOURAGE.
DR. ASHMORE, THIS IS FARRIN.
I WORK FOR THE SUMMIT ORGANIZERS. WE ARE VERY SORRY TO HEAR OF THE VANDALISM TO YOUR LUGGAGE. MAY I RIDE WITH YOU BACK TO THE HOTEL?
NO STOPPING IN RED ZONE
THIS SECURITY BREACH IS UNACCEPTABLE. WE HAVE A LOT OF PASSIONATE PEOPLE AT THIS SUMMIT, REPRESENTING VIEWS FROM ACROSS THE POLITICAL SPECTRUM.
DESTROYING PROPERTY DOES NOT BELONG ANYWHERE ON THE SPECTRUM.
POLITICAL SPECTRUM? ANOTHER ONE OF DAD'S YAWN-FESTS. WAKE ME WHEN WE'RE AT THE HOTEL.
THE POLITICAL SPECTRUM AFFECTS EVERY DECISION MADE ABOUT HOW TO RUN A COUNTRY. AND IT COULD HELP US FIND OUT WHO SLICED YOUR DAD'S BAGS.

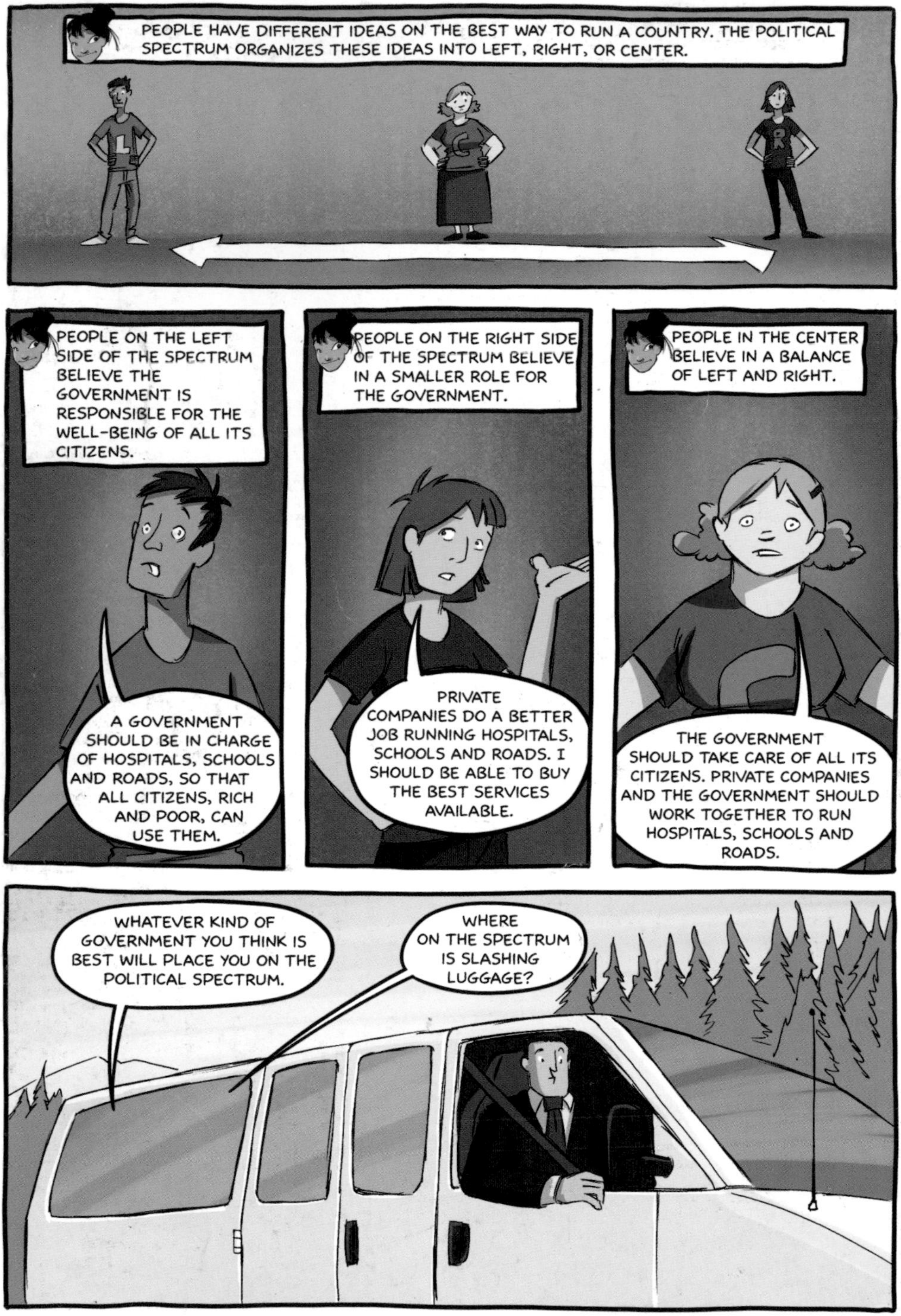
PEOPLE HAVE DIFFERENT IDEAS ON THE BEST WAY TO RUN A COUNTRY. THE POLITICAL SPECTRUM ORGANIZES THESE IDEAS INTO LEFT, RIGHT, OR CENTER.
PEOPLE ON THE LEFT SIDE OF THE SPECTRUM BELIEVE THE GOVERNMENT IS RESPONSIBLE FOR THE WELL-BEING OF ALL ITS CITIZENS.
A GOVERNMENT SHOULD BE IN CHARGE OF HOSPITALS, SCHOOLS AND ROADS, SO THAT ALL CITIZENS, RICH AND POOR, CAN USE THEM.
PEOPLE ON THE RIGHT SIDE OF THE SPECTRUM BELIEVE IN A SMALLER ROLE FOR THE GOVERNMENT.
PRIVATE COMPANIES DO A BETTER JOB RUNNING HOSPITALS, SCHOOLS AND ROADS. I SHOULD BE ABLE TO BUY THE BEST SERVICES AVAILABLE.
PEOPLE IN THE CENTER BELIEVE IN A BALANCE OF LEFT AND RIGHT.
THE GOVERNMENT SHOULD TAKE CARE OF ALL ITS CITIZENS. PRIVATE COMPANIES AND THE GOVERNMENT SHOULD WORK TOGETHER TO RUN HOSPITALS, SCHOOLS AND ROADS.
WHATEVER KIND OF GOVERNMENT YOU THINK IS BEST WILL PLACE YOU ON THE POLITICAL SPECTRUM.
WHERE ON THE SPECTRUM IS SLASHING LUGGAGE?

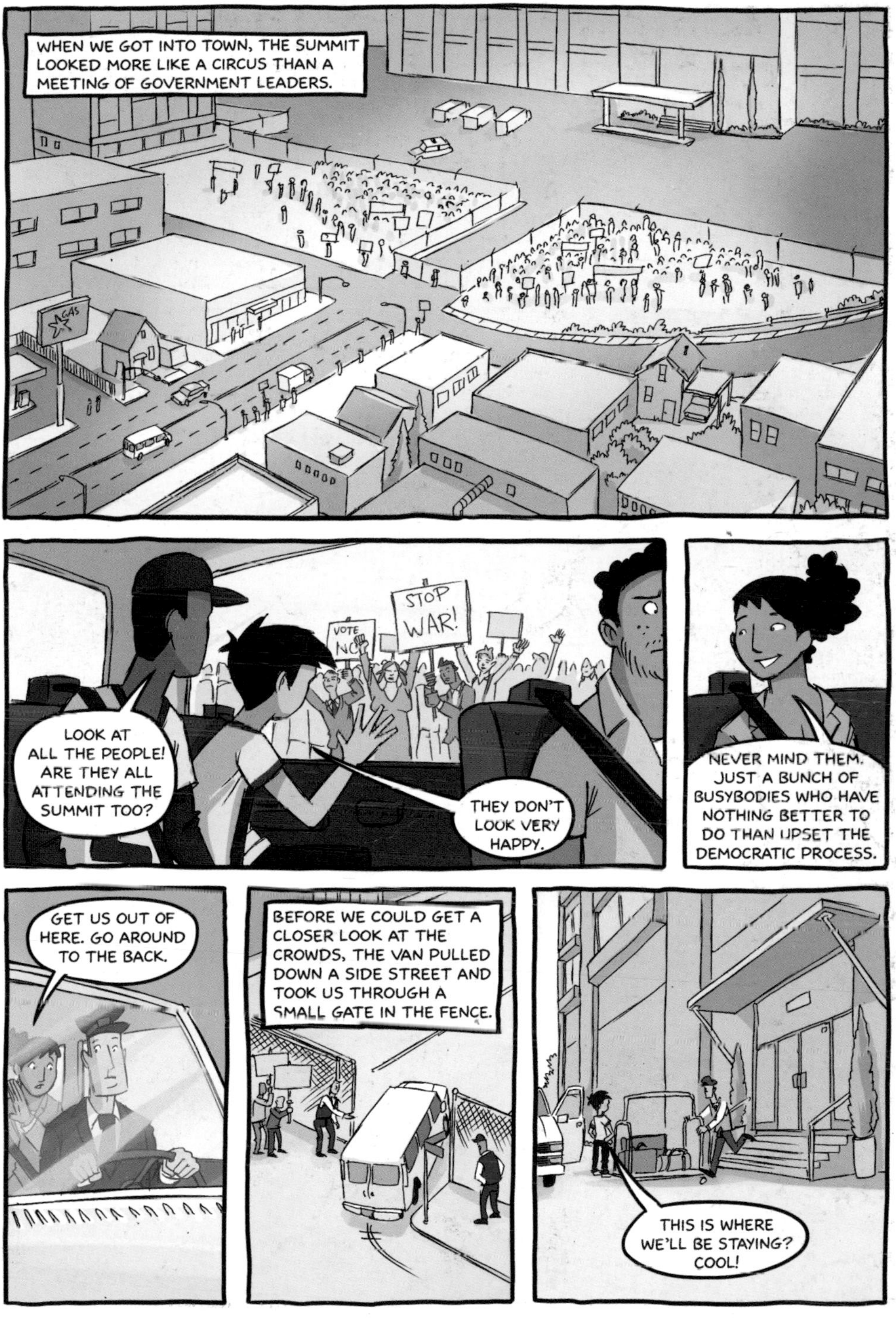
WHEN WE GOT INTO TOWN, THE SUMMIT LOOKED MORE LIKE A CIRCUS THAN A MEETING OF GOVERNMENT LEADERS.
GAS
STOP WAR!
VOTE NO
LOOK AT ALL THE PEOPLE! ARE THEY ALL ATTENDING THE SUMMIT TOO?
THEY DON'T LOOK VERY HAPPY.
NEVER MIND THEM. JUST A BUNCH OF BUSYBODIES WHO HAVE NOTHING BETTER TO DO THAN UPSET THE DEMOCRATIC PROCESS.
GET US OUT OF HERE. GO AROUND TO THE BACK.
BEFORE WE COULD GET A CLOSER LOOK AT THE CROWDS, THE VAN PULLED DOWN A SIDE STREET AND TOOK US THROUGH A SMALL GATE IN THE FENCE.
THIS IS WHERE WE'LL BE STAYING? COOL!

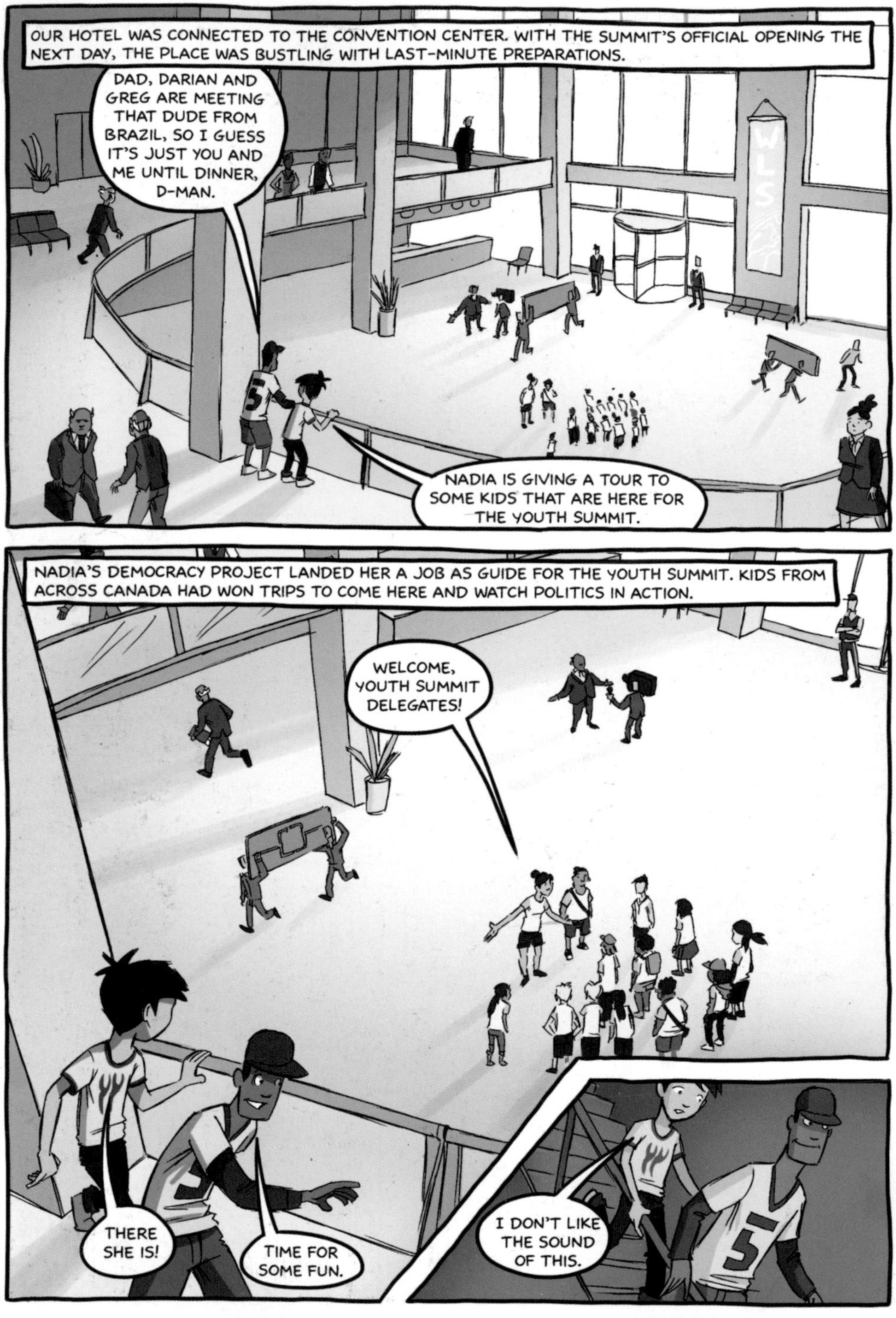
OUR HOTEL WAS CONNECTED TO THE CONVENTION CENTER. WITH THE SUMMIT'S OFFICIAL OPENING THE NEXT DAY, THE PLACE WAS BUSTLING WITH LAST-MINUTE PREPARATIONS.
DAD, DARIAN AND GREG ARE MEETING THAT DUDE FROM BRAZIL, SO I GUESS IT'S JUST YOU AND ME UNTIL DINNER, D-MAN.
WLS
NADIA IS GIVING A TOUR TO SOME KIDS THAT ARE HERE FOR THE YOUTH SUMMIT.
NADIA'S DEMOCRACY PROJECT LANDED HER A JOB AS GUIDE FOR THE YOUTH SUMMIT. KIDS FROM ACROSS CANADA HAD WON TRIPS TO COME HERE AND WATCH POLITICS IN ACTION.
WELCOME, YOUTH SUMMIT DELEGATES!
THERE SHE IS!
TIME FOR SOME FUN.
I DON'T LIKE THE SOUND OF THIS.

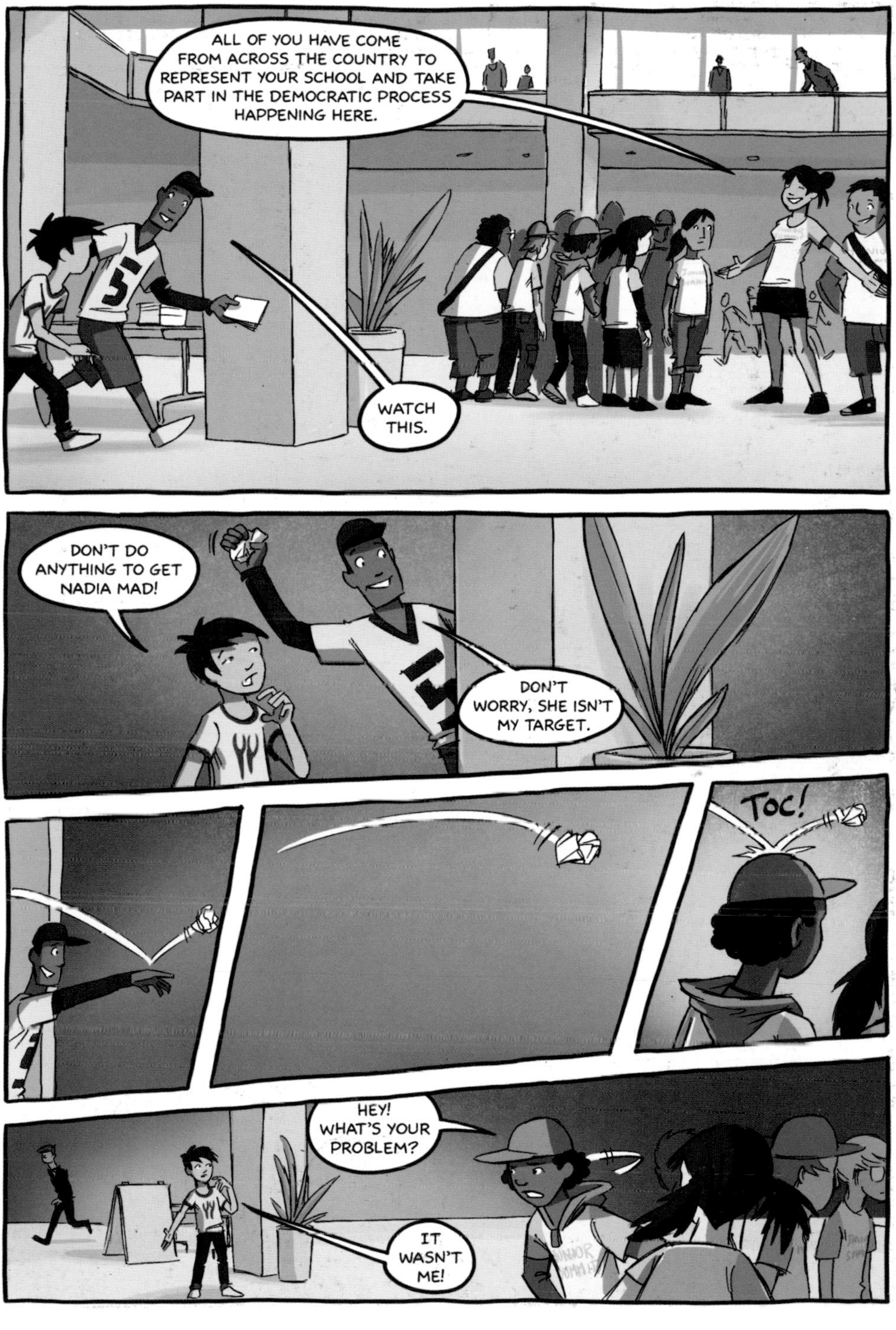
ALL OF YOU HAVE COME FROM ACROSS THE COUNTRY TO REPRESENT YOUR SCHOOL AND TAKE PART IN THE DEMOCRATIC PROCESS HAPPENING HERE.
WATCH THIS.
DON'T DO ANYTHING TO GET NADIA MAD!
DON'T WORRY, SHE ISN'T MY TARGET.
TOC!
HEY! WHAT'S YOUR PROBLEM?
IT WASN'T ME!

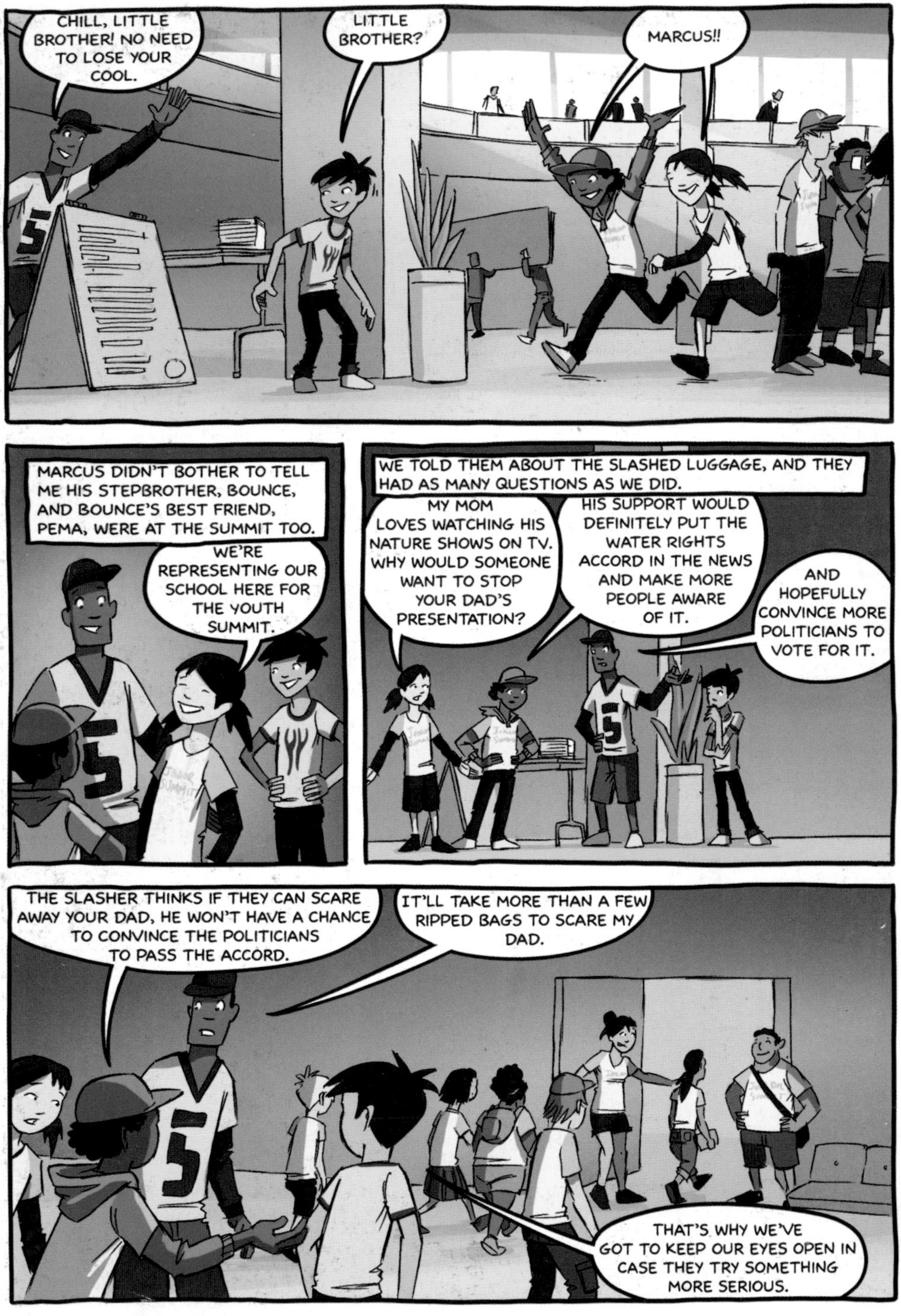
CHILL, LITTLE BROTHER! NO NEED TO LOSE YOUR COOL.
LITTLE BROTHER?
MARCUS!!
MARCUS DIDN'T BOTHER TO TELL ME HIS STEPBROTHER, BOUNCE, AND BOUNCE'S BEST FRIEND, PEMA, WERE AT THE SUMMIT TOO.
WE'RE REPRESENTING OUR SCHOOL HERE FOR THE YOUTH SUMMIT.
WE TOLD THEM ABOUT THE SLASHED LUGGAGE, AND THEY HAD AS MANY QUESTIONS AS WE DID.
MY MOM LOVES WATCHING HIS NATURE SHOWS ON TV. WHY WOULD SOMEONE WANT TO STOP YOUR DAD'S PRESENTATION?
HIS SUPPORT WOULD DEFINITELY PUT THE WATER RIGHTS ACCORD IN THE NEWS AND MAKE MORE PEOPLE AWARE OF IT.
AND HOPEFULLY CONVINCE MORE POLITICIANS TO VOTE FOR IT.
THE SLASHER THINKS IF THEY CAN SCARE AWAY YOUR DAD, HE WON'T HAVE A CHANCE TO CONVINCE THE POLITICIANS TO PASS THE ACCORD.
IT'LL TAKE MORE THAN A FEW RIPPED BAGS TO SCARE MY DAD.
THAT'S WHY WE'VE GOT TO KEEP OUR EYES OPEN IN CASE THEY TRY SOMETHING MORE SERIOUS.

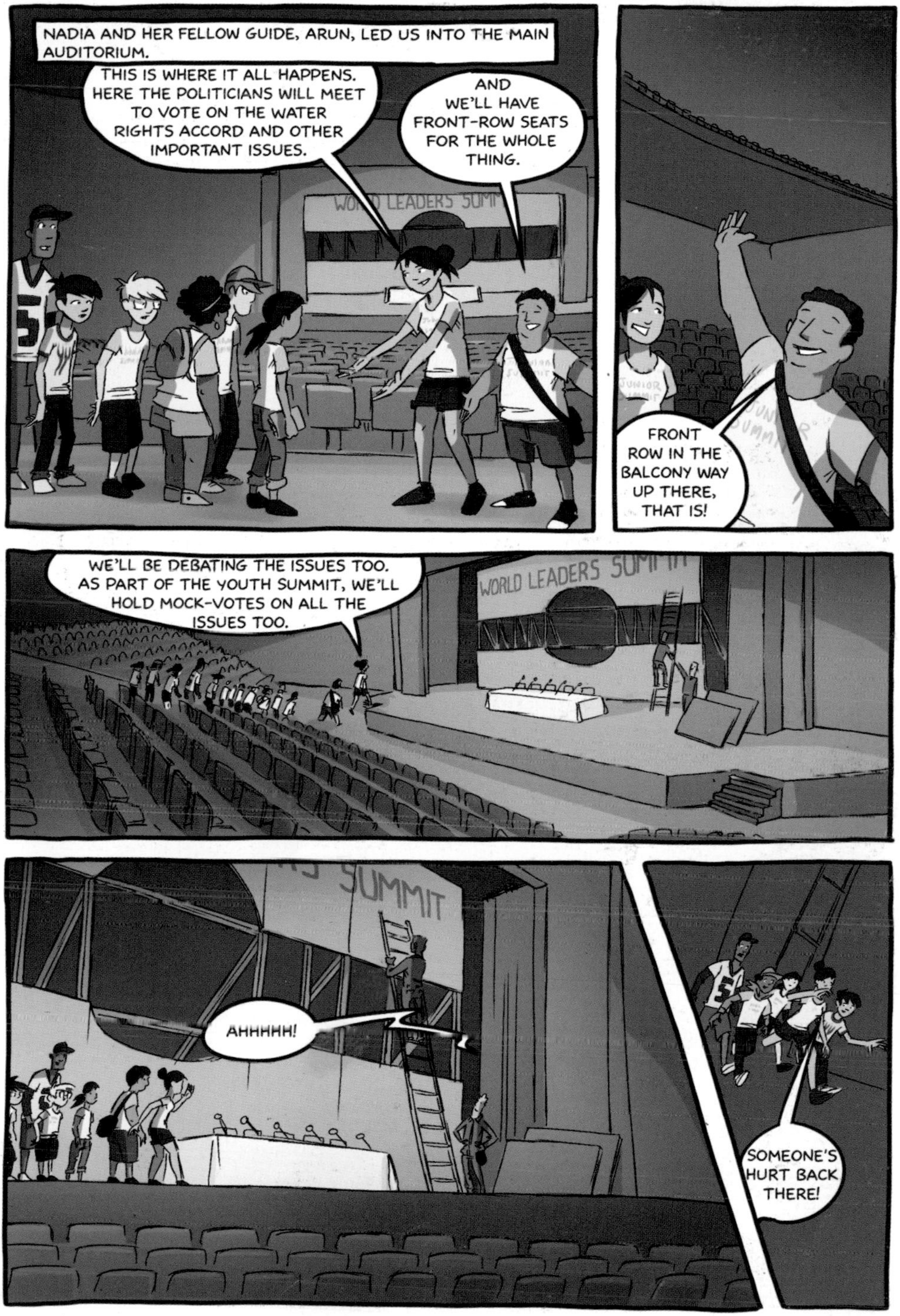
NADIA AND HER FELLOW GUIDE, ARUN, LED US INTO THE MAIN AUDITORIUM.
THIS IS WHERE IT ALL HAPPENS. HERE THE POLITICIANS WILL MEET TO VOTE ON THE WATER RIGHTS ACCORD AND OTHER IMPORTANT ISSUES.
AND WE'LL HAVE FRONT-ROW SEATS FOR THE WHOLE THING.
WORLD LEADERS SUMMIT
FRONT ROW IN THE BALCONY WAY UP THERE, THAT IS!
WE'LL BE DEBATING THE ISSUES TOO. AS PART OF THE YOUTH SUMMIT, WE'LL HOLD MOCK-VOTES ON ALL THE ISSUES TOO.
WORLD LEADERS SUMMIT
SUMMIT
AHHHHH!
SOMEONE'S HURT BACK THERE!

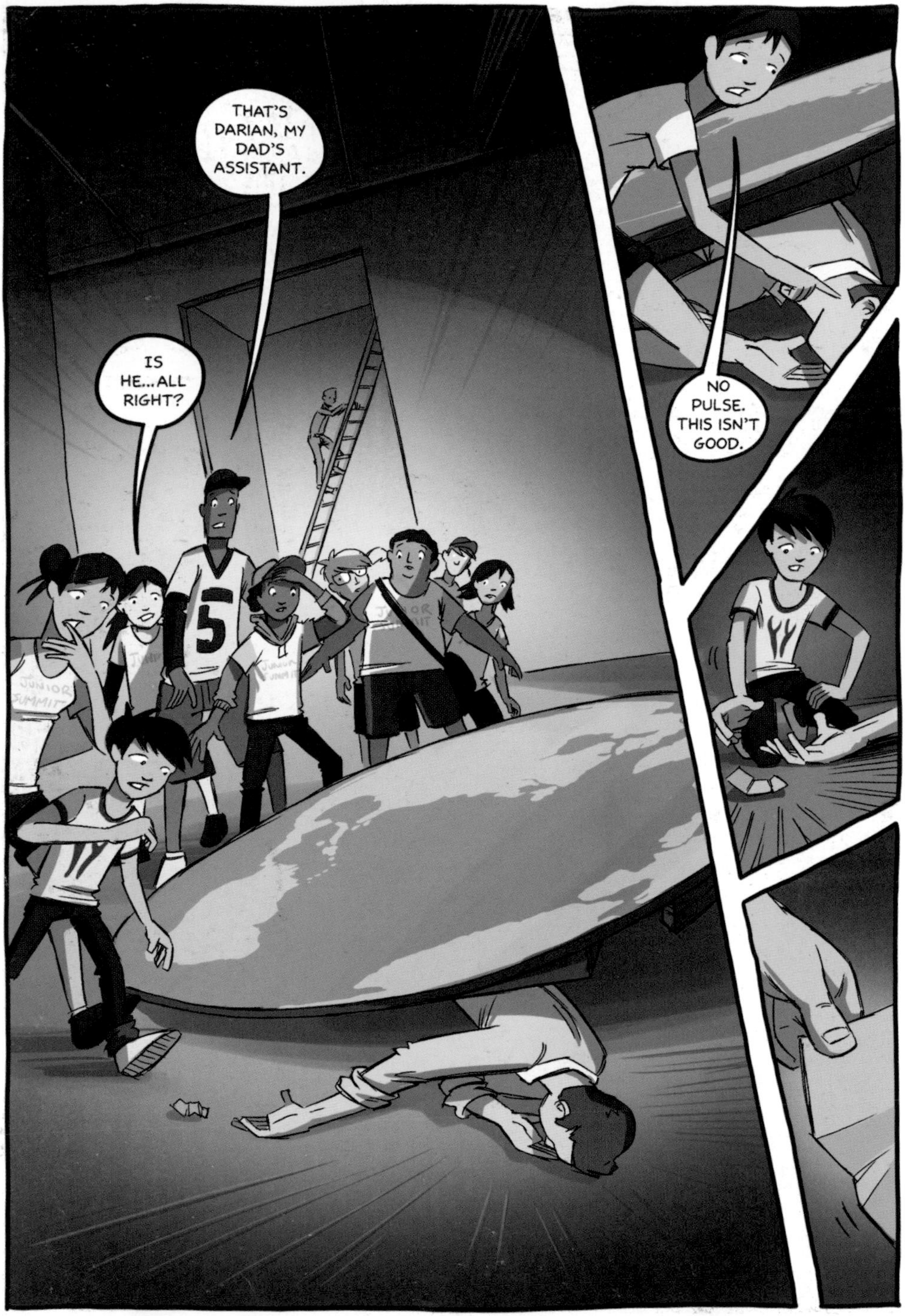
THAT'S DARIAN, MY DAD'S ASSISTANT.
IS HE...ALL RIGHT?
NO PULSE. THIS ISN'T GOOD.

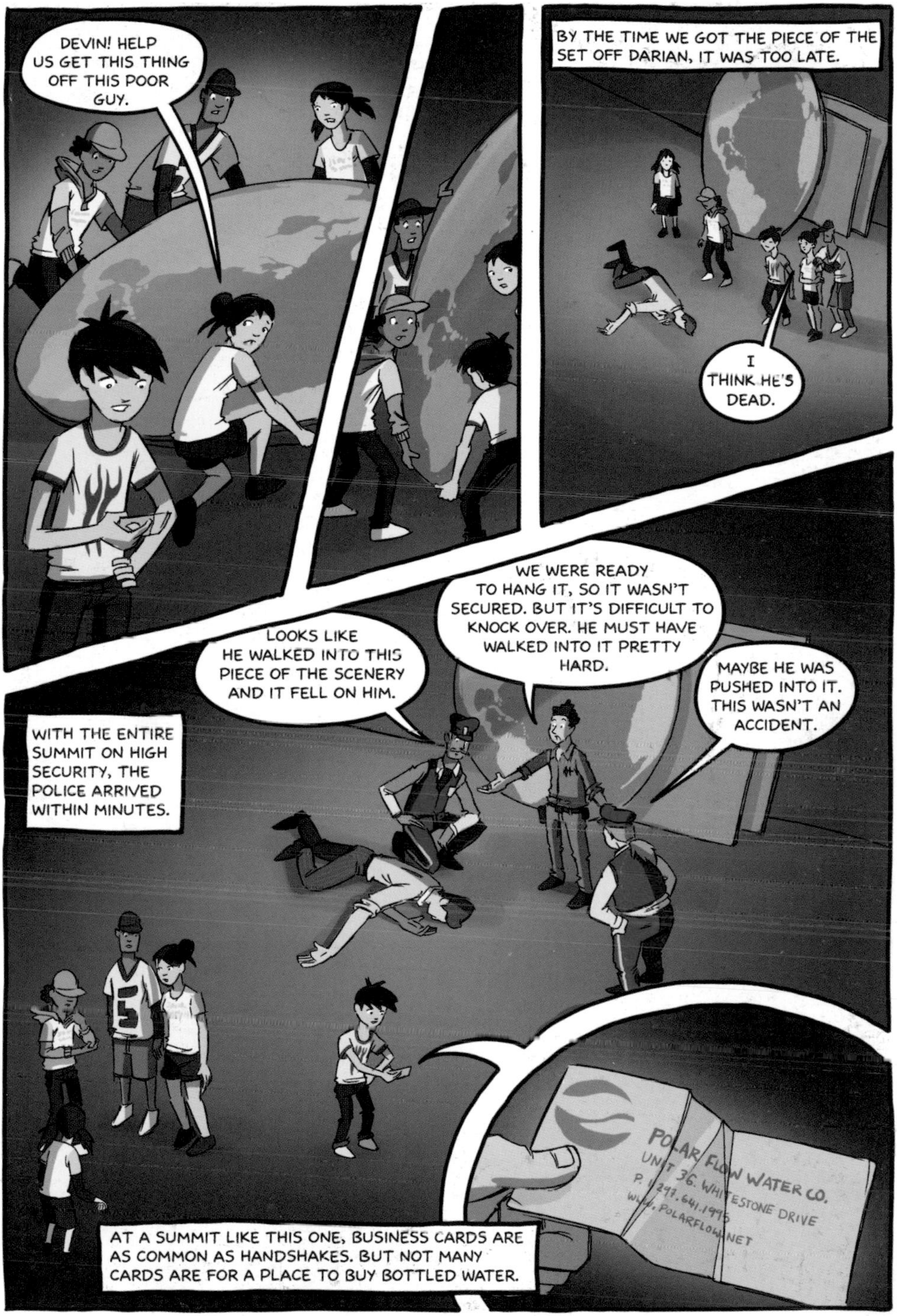
DEVIN! HELP US GET THIS THING OFF THIS POOR GUY.
BY THE TIME WE GOT THE PIECE OF THE SET OFF DARIAN, IT WAS TOO LATE.
I THINK HE'S DEAD.
WITH THE ENTIRE SUMMIT ON HIGH SECURITY, THE POLICE ARRIVED WITHIN MINUTES.
LOOKS LIKE HE WALKED INTO THIS PIECE OF THE SCENERY AND IT FELL ON HIM.
WE WERE READY TO HANG IT, SO IT WASN'T SECURED. BUT IT'S DIFFICULT TO KNOCK OVER. HE MUST HAVE WALKED INTO IT PRETTY HARD.
MAYBE HE WAS PUSHED INTO IT. THIS WASN'T AN ACCIDENT.
POLAR FLOW WATER CO.
UNIT 36. WHITESTONE DRIVE
P. 1.297.641.1995
WWW.POLARFLOW.NET
AT A SUMMIT LIKE THIS ONE, BUSINESS CARDS ARE AS COMMON AS HANDSHAKES. BUT NOT MANY CARDS ARE FOR A PLACE TO BUY BOTTLED WATER.

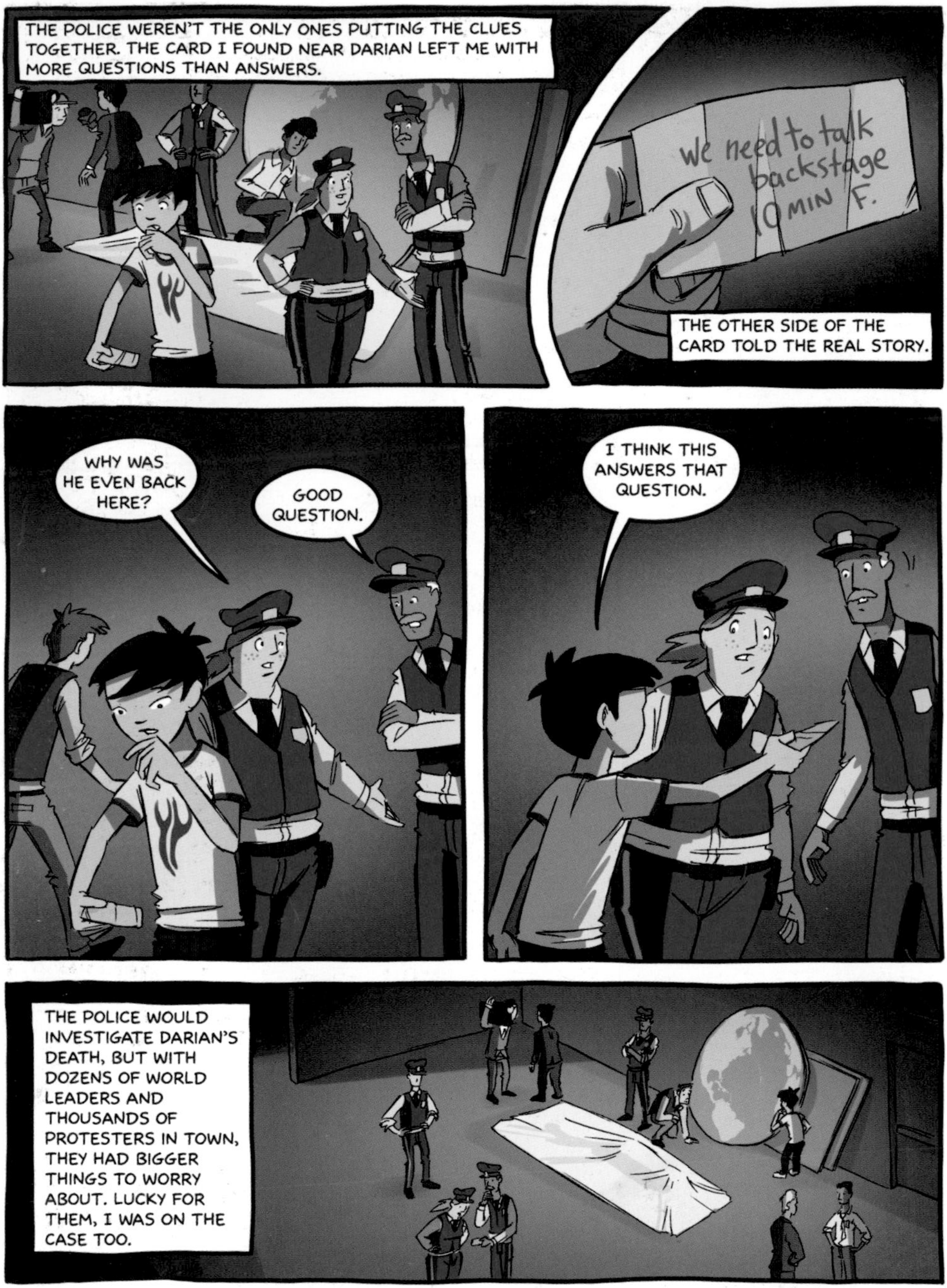
THE POLICE WEREN'T THE ONLY ONES PUTTING THE CLUES TOGETHER. THE CARD I FOUND NEAR DARIAN LEFT ME WITH MORE QUESTIONS THAN ANSWERS.
we need to talk backstage 10 MIN F.
THE OTHER SIDE OF THE CARD TOLD THE REAL STORY.
WHY WAS HE EVEN BACK HERE?
GOOD QUESTION.
I THINK THIS ANSWERS THAT QUESTION.
THE POLICE WOULD INVESTIGATE DARIAN'S DEATH, BUT WITH DOZENS OF WORLD LEADERS AND THOUSANDS OF PROTESTERS IN TOWN, THEY HAD BIGGER THINGS TO WORRY ABOUT. LUCKY FOR THEM, I WAS ON THE CASE TOO.

CHAPTER 3
BEYOND THE BARRICADE

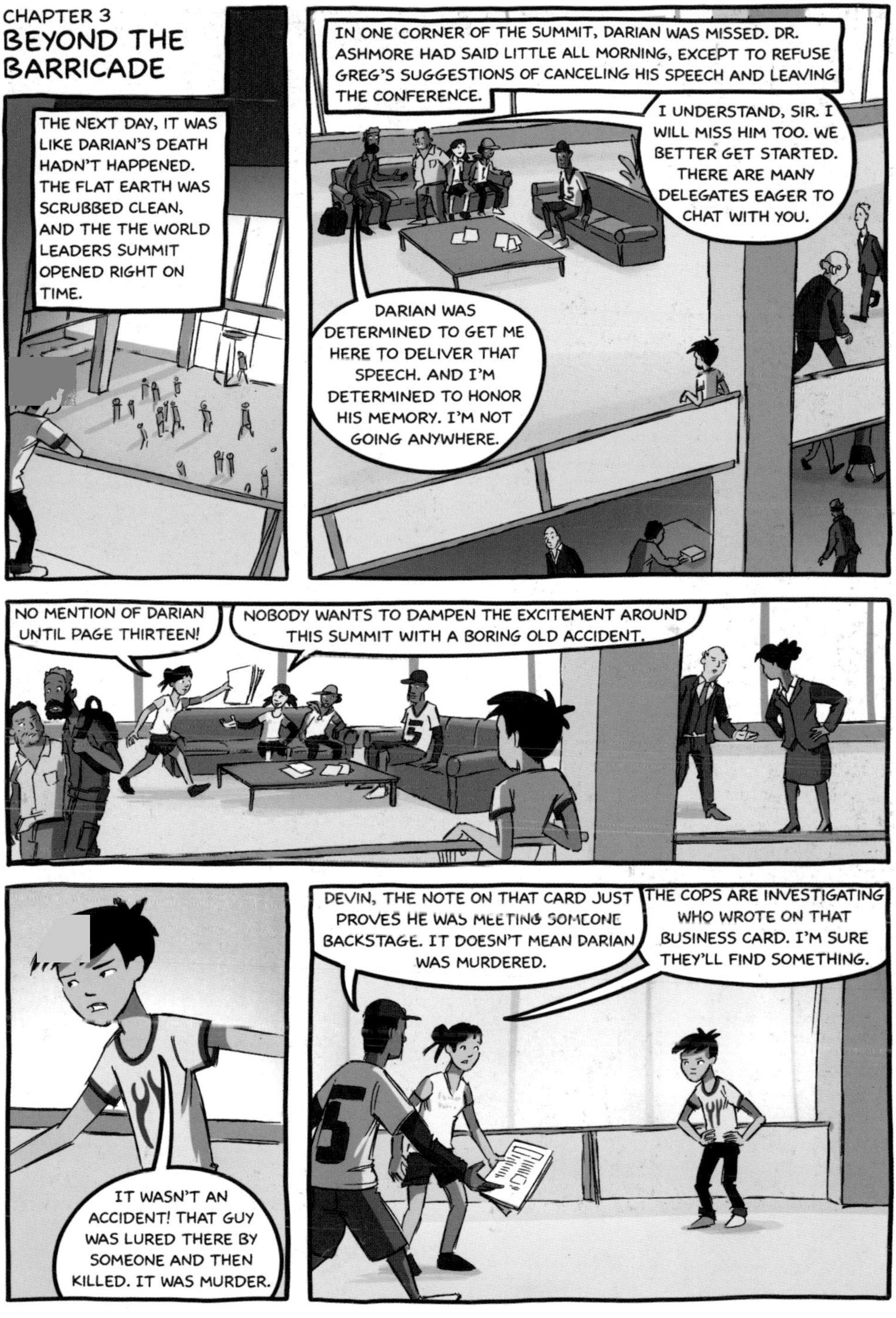
THE NEXT DAY, IT WAS LIKE DARIAN'S DEATH HADN'T HAPPENED. THE FLAT EARTH WAS SCRUBBED CLEAN, AND THE THE WORLD LEADERS SUMMIT OPENED RIGHT ON TIME.
IN ONE CORNER OF THE SUMMIT, DARIAN WAS MISSED. DR. ASHMORE HAD SAID LITTLE ALL MORNING, EXCEPT TO REFUSE GREG'S SUGGESTIONS OF CANCELING HIS SPEECH AND LEAVING THE CONFERENCE.
I UNDERSTAND, SIR. I WILL MISS HIM TOO. WE BETTER GET STARTED. THERE ARE MANY DELEGATES EAGER TO CHAT WITH YOU.
DARIAN WAS DETERMINED TO GET ME HERE TO DELIVER THAT SPEECH. AND I'M DETERMINED TO HONOR HIS MEMORY. I'M NOT GOING ANYWHERE.
NO MENTION OF DARIAN UNTIL PAGE THIRTEEN!
NOBODY WANTS TO DAMPEN THE EXCITEMENT AROUND THIS SUMMIT WITH A BORING OLD ACCIDENT.
IT WASN'T AN ACCIDENT! THAT GUY WAS LURED THERE BY SOMEONE AND THEN KILLED. IT WAS MURDER.
DEVIN, THE NOTE ON THAT CARD JUST PROVES HE WAS MEETING SOMEONE BACKSTAGE. IT DOESN'T MEAN DARIAN WAS MURDERED.
THE COPS ARE INVESTIGATING WHO WROTE ON THAT BUSINESS CARD. I'M SURE THEY'LL FIND SOMETHING.

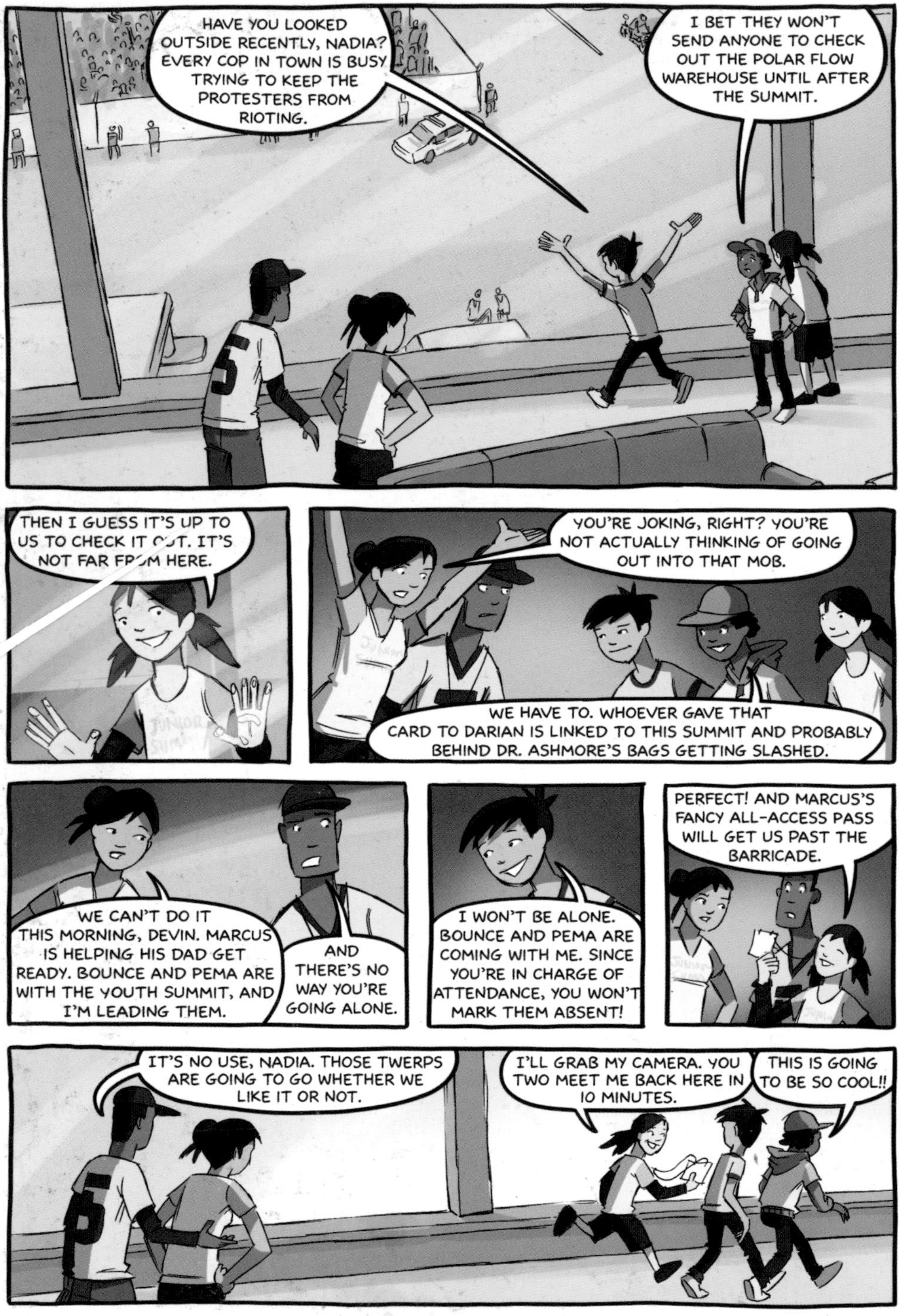
HAVE YOU LOOKED OUTSIDE RECENTLY, NADIA? EVERY COP IN TOWN IS BUSY TRYING TO KEEP THE PROTESTERS FROM RIOTING.
I BET THEY WON'T SEND ANYONE TO CHECK OUT THE POLAR FLOW WAREHOUSE UNTIL AFTER THE SUMMIT.
THEN I GUESS IT'S UP TO US TO CHECK IT OUT. IT'S NOT FAR FROM HERE.
YOU'RE JOKING, RIGHT? YOU'RE NOT ACTUALLY THINKING OF GOING OUT INTO THAT MOB.
WE HAVE TO. WHOEVER GAVE THAT CARD TO DARIAN IS LINKED TO THIS SUMMIT AND PROBABLY BEHIND DR. ASHMORE'S BAGS GETTING SLASHED.
WE CAN'T DO IT THIS MORNING, DEVIN. MARCUS IS HELPING HIS DAD GET READY. BOUNCE AND PEMA ARE WITH THE YOUTH SUMMIT, AND I'M LEADING THEM.
AND THERE'S NO WAY YOU'RE GOING ALONE.
I WON'T BE ALONE. BOUNCE AND PEMA ARE COMING WITH ME. SINCE YOU'RE IN CHARGE OF ATTENDANCE, YOU WON'T MARK THEM ABSENT!
PERFECT! AND MARCUS'S FANCY ALL-ACCESS PASS WILL GET US PAST THE BARRICADE.
IT'S NO USE, NADIA. THOSE TWERPS ARE GOING TO GO WHETHER WE LIKE IT OR NOT.
I'LL GRAB MY CAMERA. YOU TWO MEET ME BACK HERE IN 10 MINUTES.
THIS IS GOING TO BE SO COOL!!

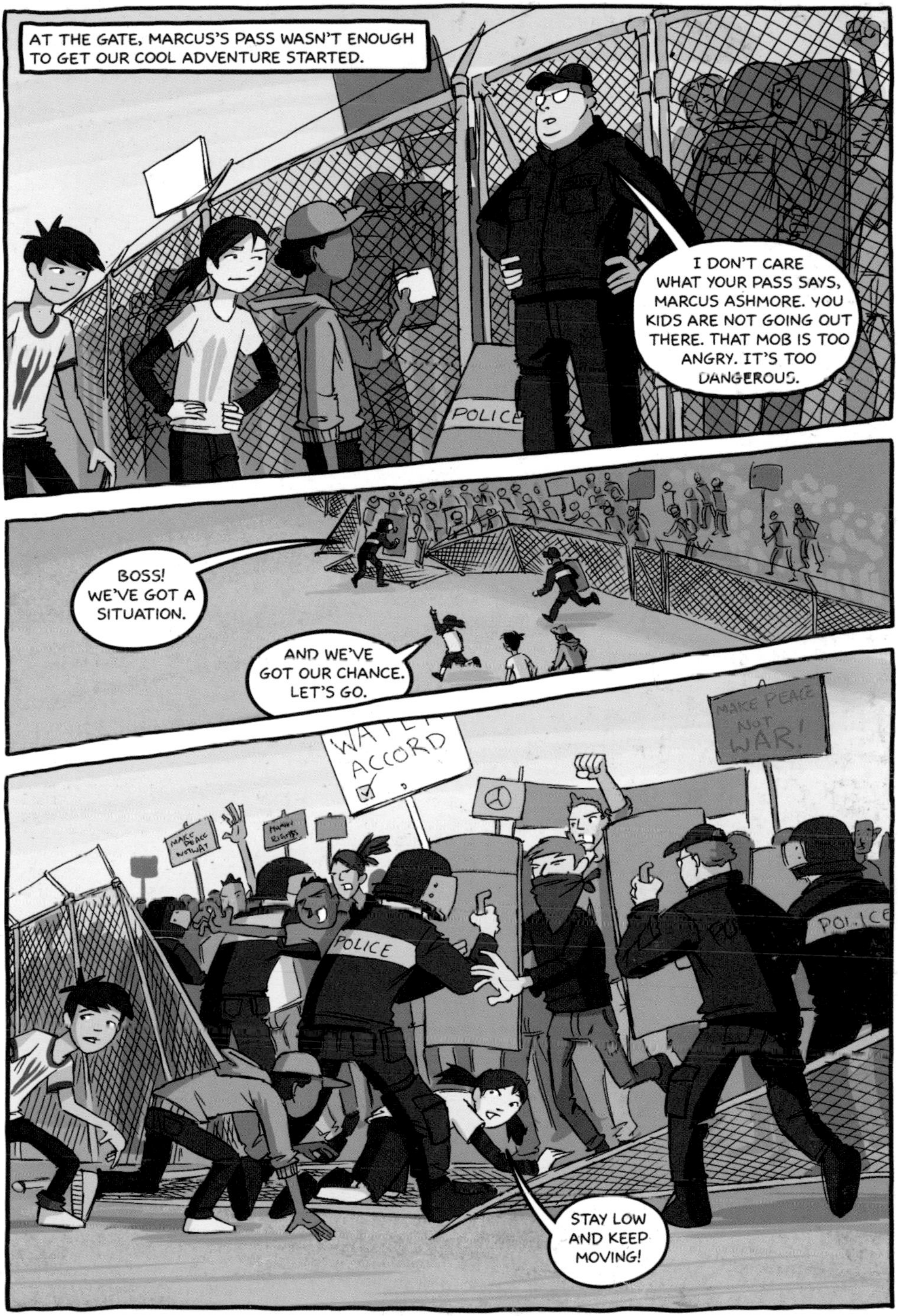
AT THE GATE, MARCUS'S PASS WASN'T ENOUGH TO GET OUR COOL ADVENTURE STARTED.
I DON'T CARE WHAT YOUR PASS SAYS, MARCUS ASHMORE. YOU KIDS ARE NOT GOING OUT THERE. THAT MOB IS TOO ANGRY. IT'S TOO DANGEROUS.
POLICE
BOSS! WE'VE GOT A SITUATION.
AND WE'VE GOT OUR CHANCE. LET'S GO.
WATER ACCORD
MAKE PEACE NOT WAR!
HUMAN RIGHTS
POLICE
POLICE
STAY LOW AND KEEP MOVING!

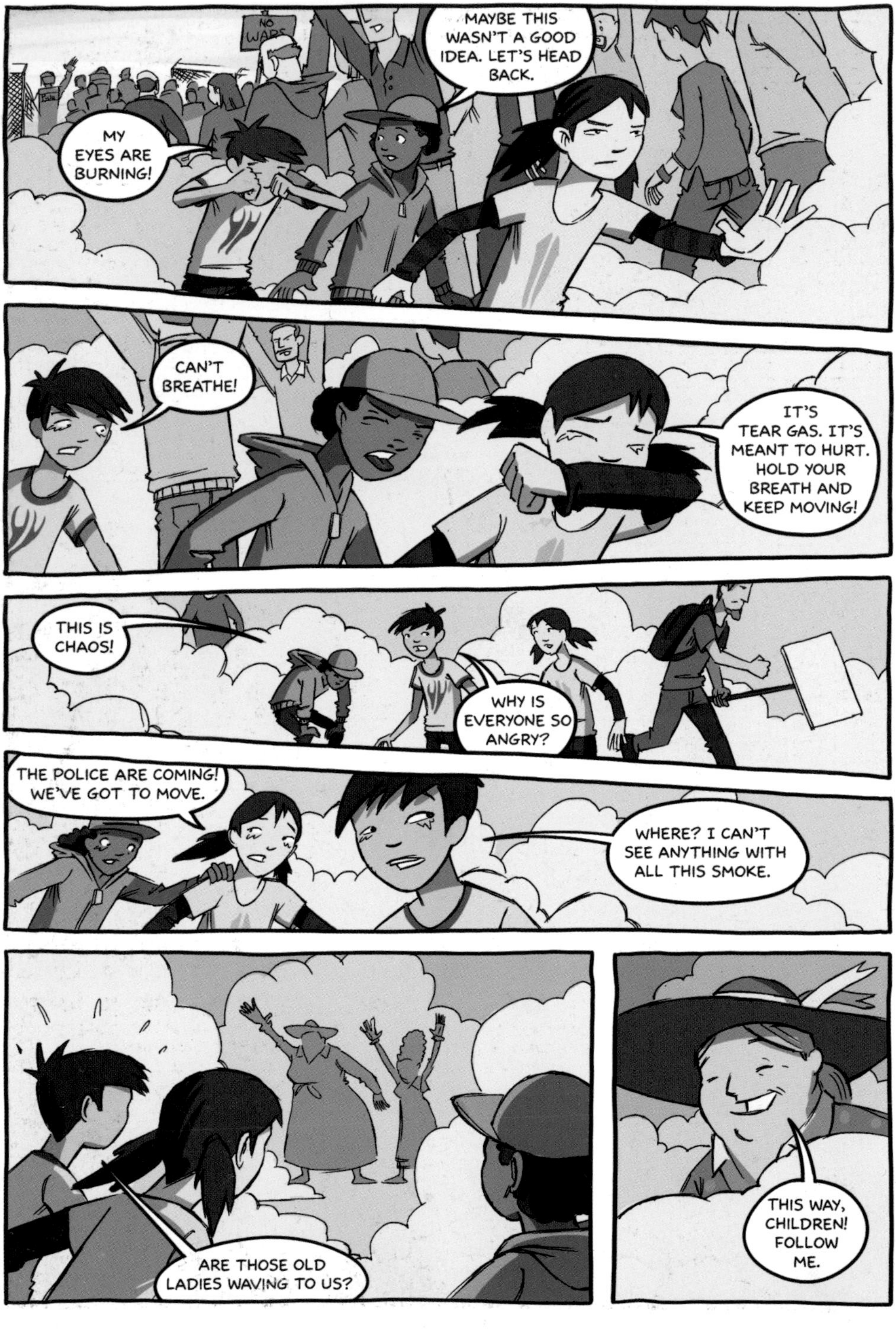
NO WARS
MAYBE THIS WASN'T A GOOD IDEA. LET'S HEAD BACK.
MY EYES ARE BURNING!
CAN'T BREATHE!
IT'S TEAR GAS. IT'S MEANT TO HURT. HOLD YOUR BREATH AND KEEP MOVING!
THIS IS CHAOS!
WHY IS EVERYONE SO ANGRY?
THE POLICE ARE COMING! WE'VE GOT TO MOVE.
WHERE? I CAN'T SEE ANYTHING WITH ALL THIS SMOKE.
ARE THOSE OLD LADIES WAVING TO US?
THIS WAY, CHILDREN! FOLLOW ME.

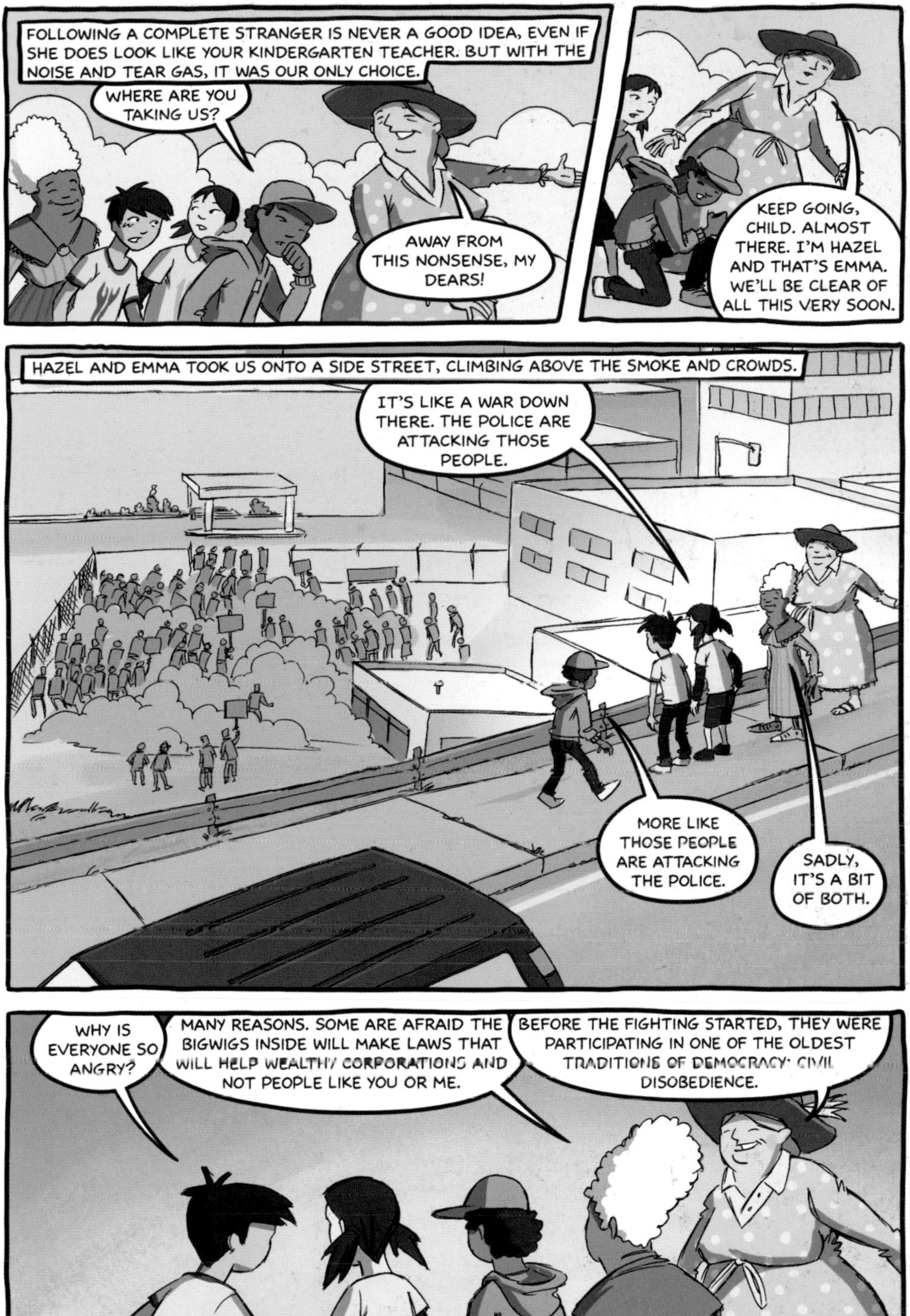
FOLLOWING A COMPLETE STRANGER IS NEVER A GOOD IDEA, EVEN IF SHE DOES LOOK LIKE YOUR KINDERGARTEN TEACHER. BUT WITH THE NOISE AND TEAR GAS, IT WAS OUR ONLY CHOICE.
WHERE ARE YOU TAKING US?
AWAY FROM THIS NONSENSE, MY DEARS!
KEEP GOING, CHILD. ALMOST THERE. I'M HAZEL AND THAT'S EMMA. WE'LL BE CLEAR OF ALL THIS VERY SOON.
HAZEL AND EMMA TOOK US ONTO A SIDE STREET, CLIMBING ABOVE THE SMOKE AND CROWDS.
IT'S LIKE A WAR DOWN THERE. THE POLICE ARE ATTACKING THOSE PEOPLE.
MORE LIKE THOSE PEOPLE ARE ATTACKING THE POLICE.
SADLY, IT'S A BIT OF BOTH.
WHY IS EVERYONE SO ANGRY?
MANY REASONS. SOME ARE AFRAID THE BIGWIGS INSIDE WILL MAKE LAWS THAT WILL HELP WEALTHY CORPORATIONS AND NOT PEOPLE LIKE YOU OR ME.
BEFORE THE FIGHTING STARTED, THEY WERE PARTICIPATING IN ONE OF THE OLDEST TRADITIONS OF DEMOCRACY: CIVIL DISOBEDIENCE.

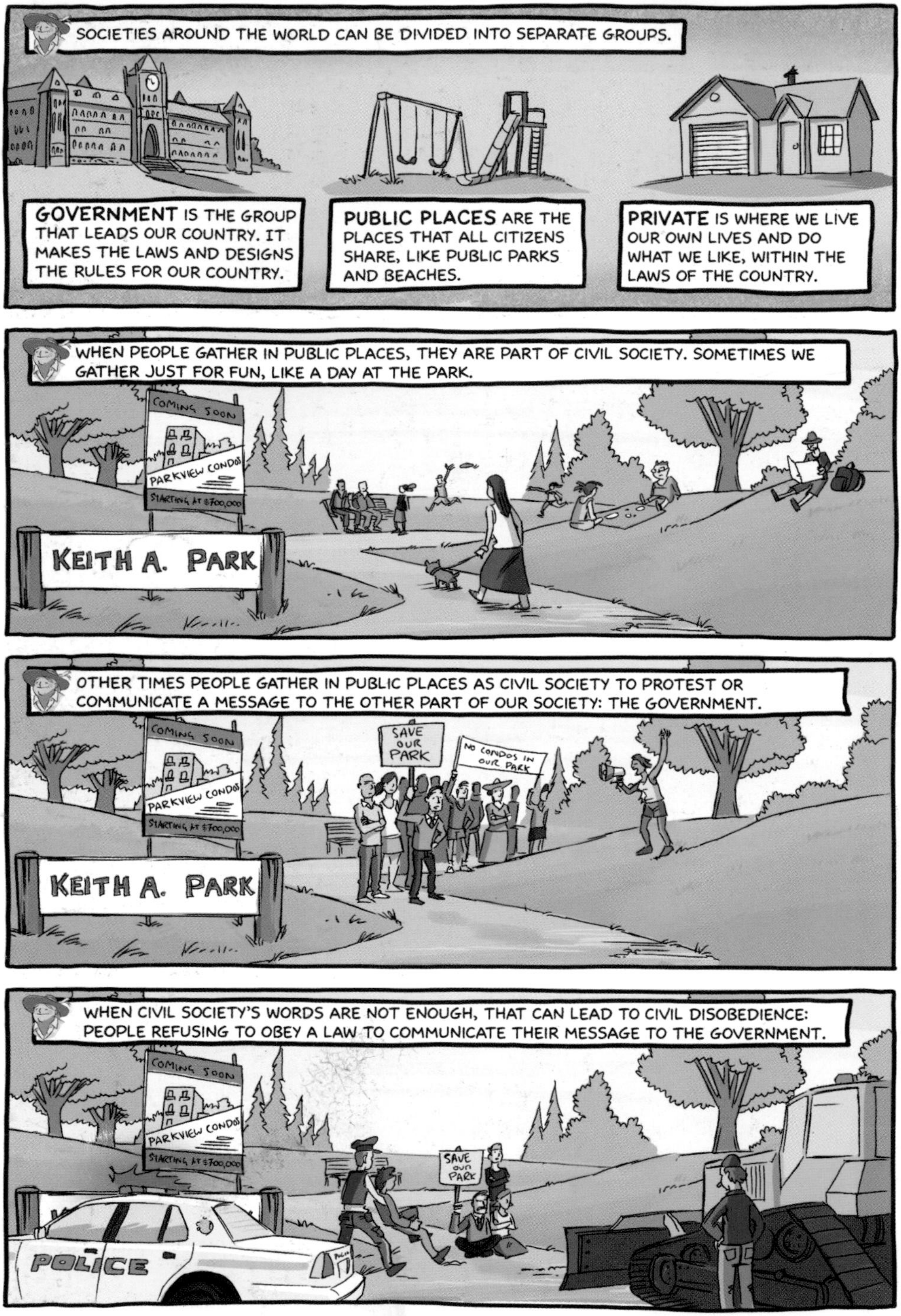
SOCIETIES AROUND THE WORLD CAN BE DIVIDED INTO SEPARATE GROUPS.
GOVERNMENT IS THE GROUP THAT LEADS OUR COUNTRY. IT MAKES THE LAWS AND DESIGNS THE RULES FOR OUR COUNTRY.
PUBLIC PLACES ARE THE PLACES THAT ALL CITIZENS SHARE, LIKE PUBLIC PARKS AND BEACHES.
PRIVATE IS WHERE WE LIVE OUR OWN LIVES AND DO WHAT WE LIKE, WITHIN THE LAWS OF THE COUNTRY.
WHEN PEOPLE GATHER IN PUBLIC PLACES, THEY ARE PART OF CIVIL SOCIETY. SOMETIMES WE GATHER JUST FOR FUN, LIKE A DAY AT THE PARK.
COMING SOON
PARKVIEW CONDOS
STARTING AT $700,000
KEITH A. PARK
OTHER TIMES PEOPLE GATHER IN PUBLIC PLACES AS CIVIL SOCIETY TO PROTEST OR COMMUNICATE A MESSAGE TO THE OTHER PART OF OUR SOCIETY: THE GOVERNMENT.
COMING SOON
PARKVIEW CONDOS
STARTING AT $700,000
SAVE OUR PARK
NO CONDOS IN OUR PARK
KEITH A. PARK
WHEN CIVIL SOCIETY'S WORDS ARE NOT ENOUGH, THAT CAN LEAD TO CIVIL DISOBEDIENCE: PEOPLE REFUSING TO OBEY A LAW TO COMMUNICATE THEIR MESSAGE TO THE GOVERNMENT.
COMING SOON
PARKVIEW CONDOS
STARTING AT $700,000
SAVE OUR PARK
POLICE

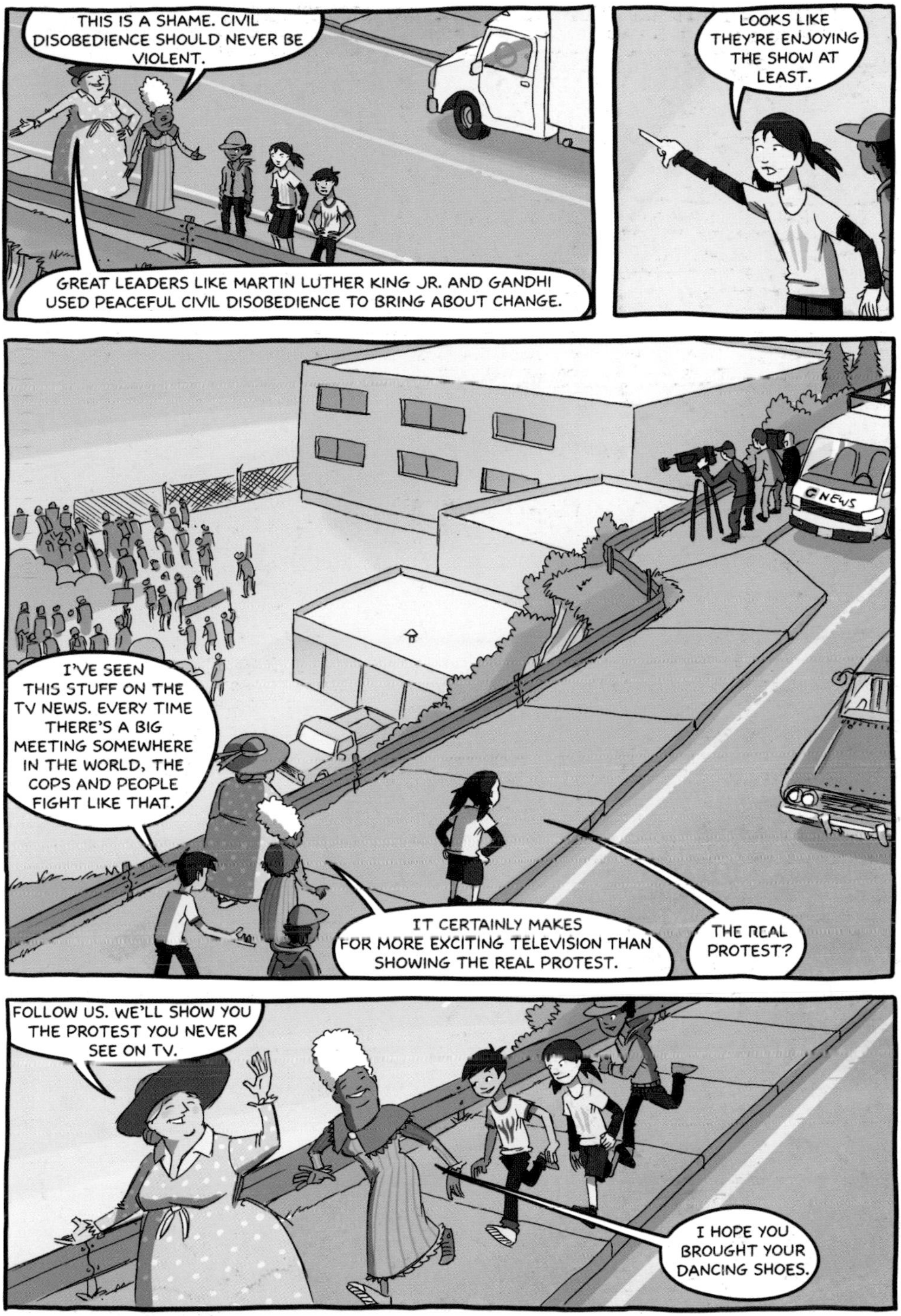
THIS IS A SHAME. CIVIL DISOBEDIENCE SHOULD NEVER BE VIOLENT.
GREAT LEADERS LIKE MARTIN LUTHER KING JR. AND GANDHI USED PEACEFUL CIVIL DISOBEDIENCE TO BRING ABOUT CHANGE.
LOOKS LIKE THEY'RE ENJOYING THE SHOW AT LEAST.
NEWS
I'VE SEEN THIS STUFF ON THE TV NEWS. EVERY TIME THERE'S A BIG MEETING SOMEWHERE IN THE WORLD, THE COPS AND PEOPLE FIGHT LIKE THAT.
IT CERTAINLY MAKES FOR MORE EXCITING TELEVISION THAN SHOWING THE REAL PROTEST.
THE REAL PROTEST?
FOLLOW US. WE'LL SHOW YOU THE PROTEST YOU NEVER SEE ON TV.
I HOPE YOU BROUGHT YOUR DANCING SHOES.

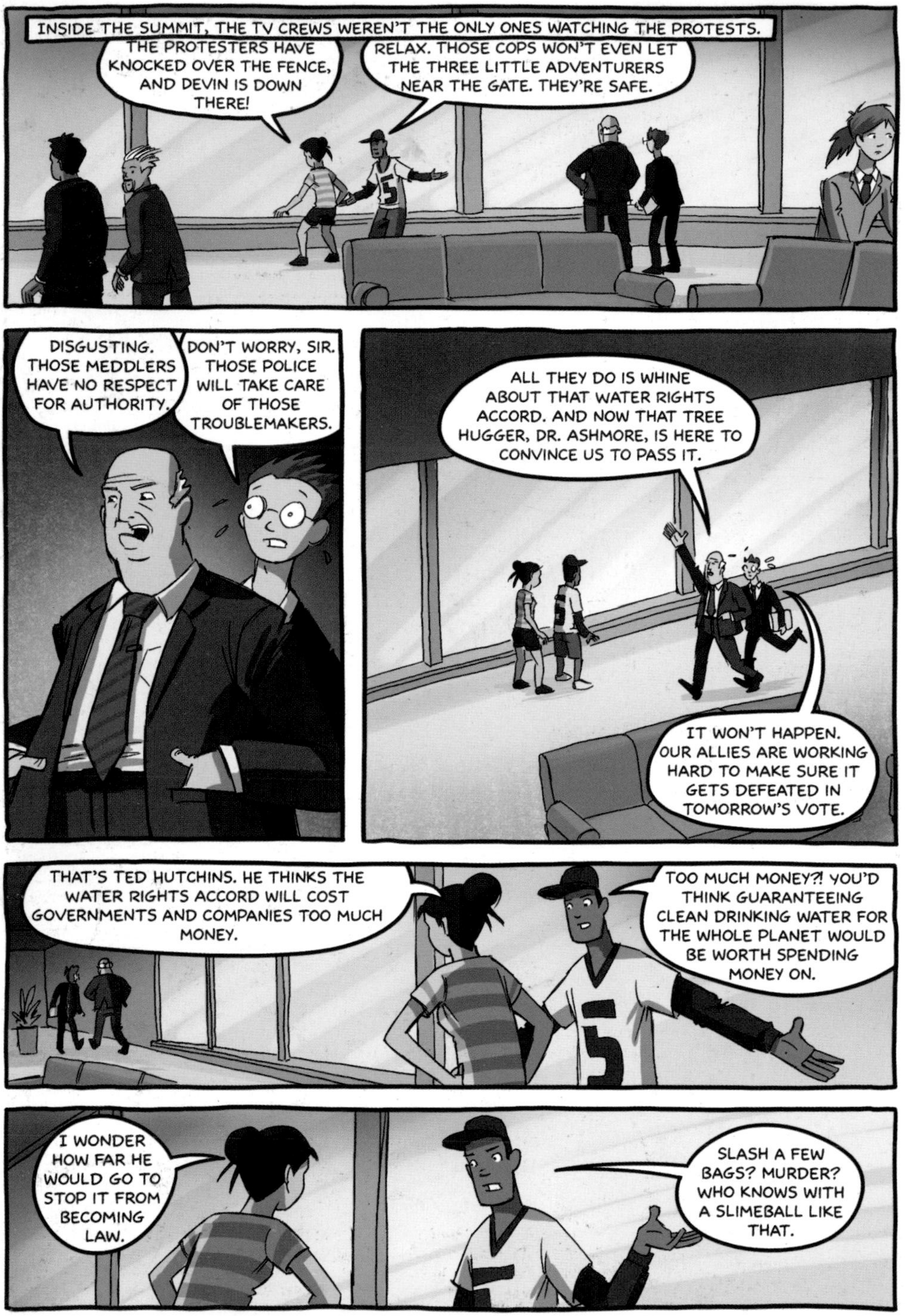
INSIDE THE SUMMIT, THE TV CREWS WEREN'T THE ONLY ONES WATCHING THE PROTESTS.
THE PROTESTERS HAVE KNOCKED OVER THE FENCE, AND DEVIN IS DOWN THERE!
RELAX. THOSE COPS WON'T EVEN LET THE THREE LITTLE ADVENTURERS NEAR THE GATE. THEY'RE SAFE.
DISGUSTING. THOSE MEDDLERS HAVE NO RESPECT FOR AUTHORITY.
DON'T WORRY, SIR. THOSE POLICE WILL TAKE CARE OF THOSE TROUBLEMAKERS.
ALL THEY DO IS WHINE ABOUT THAT WATER RIGHTS ACCORD. AND NOW THAT TREE HUGGER, DR. ASHMORE, IS HERE TO CONVINCE US TO PASS IT.
IT WON'T HAPPEN. OUR ALLIES ARE WORKING HARD TO MAKE SURE IT GETS DEFEATED IN TOMORROW'S VOTE.
THAT'S TED HUTCHINS. HE THINKS THE WATER RIGHTS ACCORD WILL COST GOVERNMENTS AND COMPANIES TOO MUCH MONEY.
TOO MUCH MONEY?! YOU'D THINK GUARANTEEING CLEAN DRINKING WATER FOR THE WHOLE PLANET WOULD BE WORTH SPENDING MONEY ON.
I WONDER HOW FAR HE WOULD GO TO STOP IT FROM BECOMING LAW.
SLASH A FEW BAGS? MURDER? WHO KNOWS WITH A SLIMEBALL LIKE THAT.

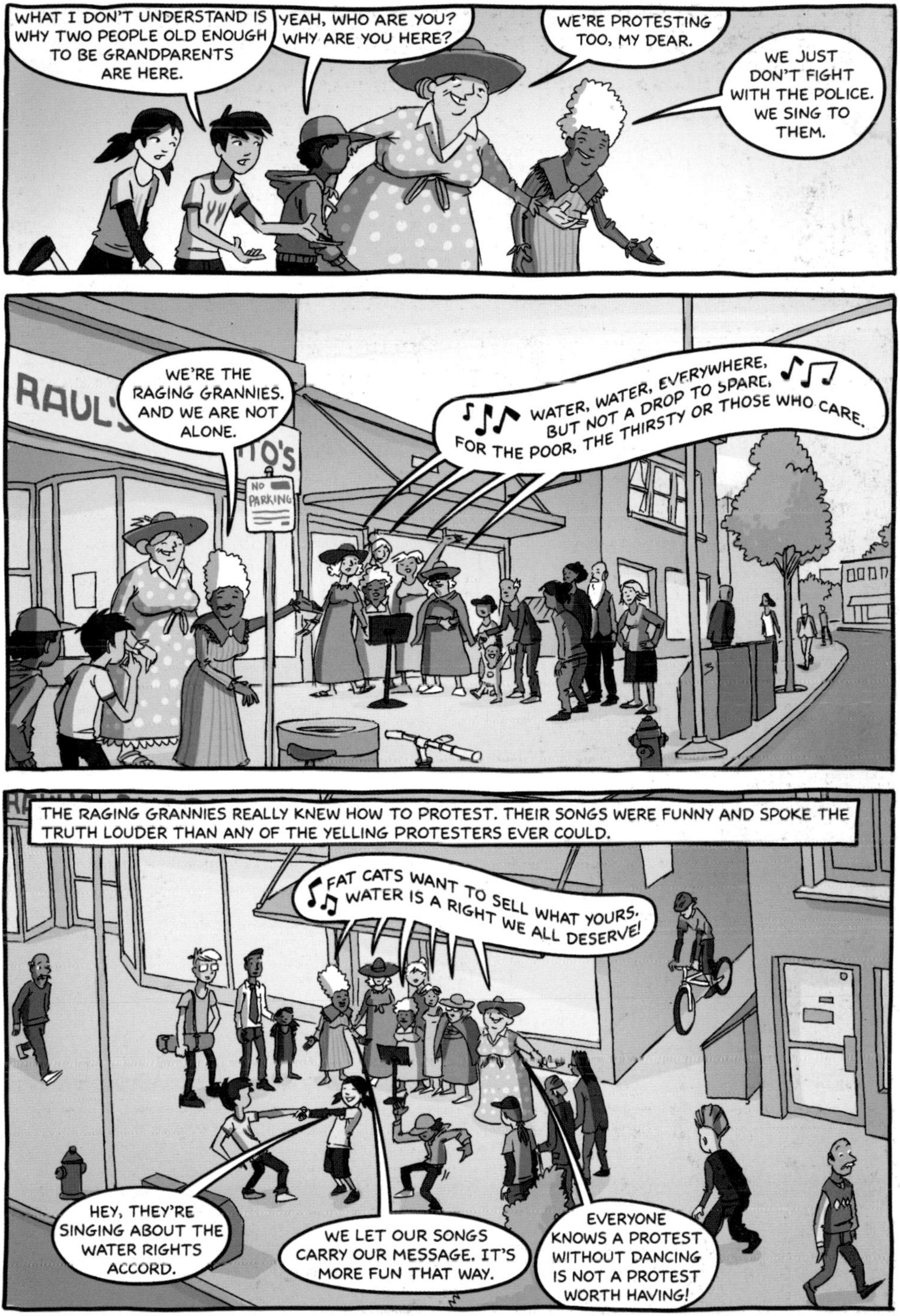
WHAT I DON'T UNDERSTAND IS WHY TWO PEOPLE OLD ENOUGH TO BE GRANDPARENTS ARE HERE.
YEAH, WHO ARE YOU? WHY ARE YOU HERE?
WE'RE PROTESTING TOO, MY DEAR.
WE JUST DON'T FIGHT WITH THE POLICE. WE SING TO THEM.
RAUL'S
NO PARKING
WE'RE THE RAGING GRANNIES. AND WE ARE NOT ALONE.
WATER, WATER, EVERYWHERE, BUT NOT A DROP TO SPARE, FOR THE POOR, THE THIRSTY OR THOSE WHO CARE.
THE RAGING GRANNIES REALLY KNEW HOW TO PROTEST. THEIR SONGS WERE FUNNY AND SPOKE THE TRUTH LOUDER THAN ANY OF THE YELLING PROTESTERS EVER COULD.
FAT CATS WANT TO SELL WHAT YOURS. WATER IS A RIGHT WE ALL DESERVE!
HEY, THEY'RE SINGING ABOUT THE WATER RIGHTS ACCORD.
WE LET OUR SONGS CARRY OUR MESSAGE. IT'S MORE FUN THAT WAY.
EVERYONE KNOWS A PROTEST WITHOUT DANCING IS NOT A PROTEST WORTH HAVING!

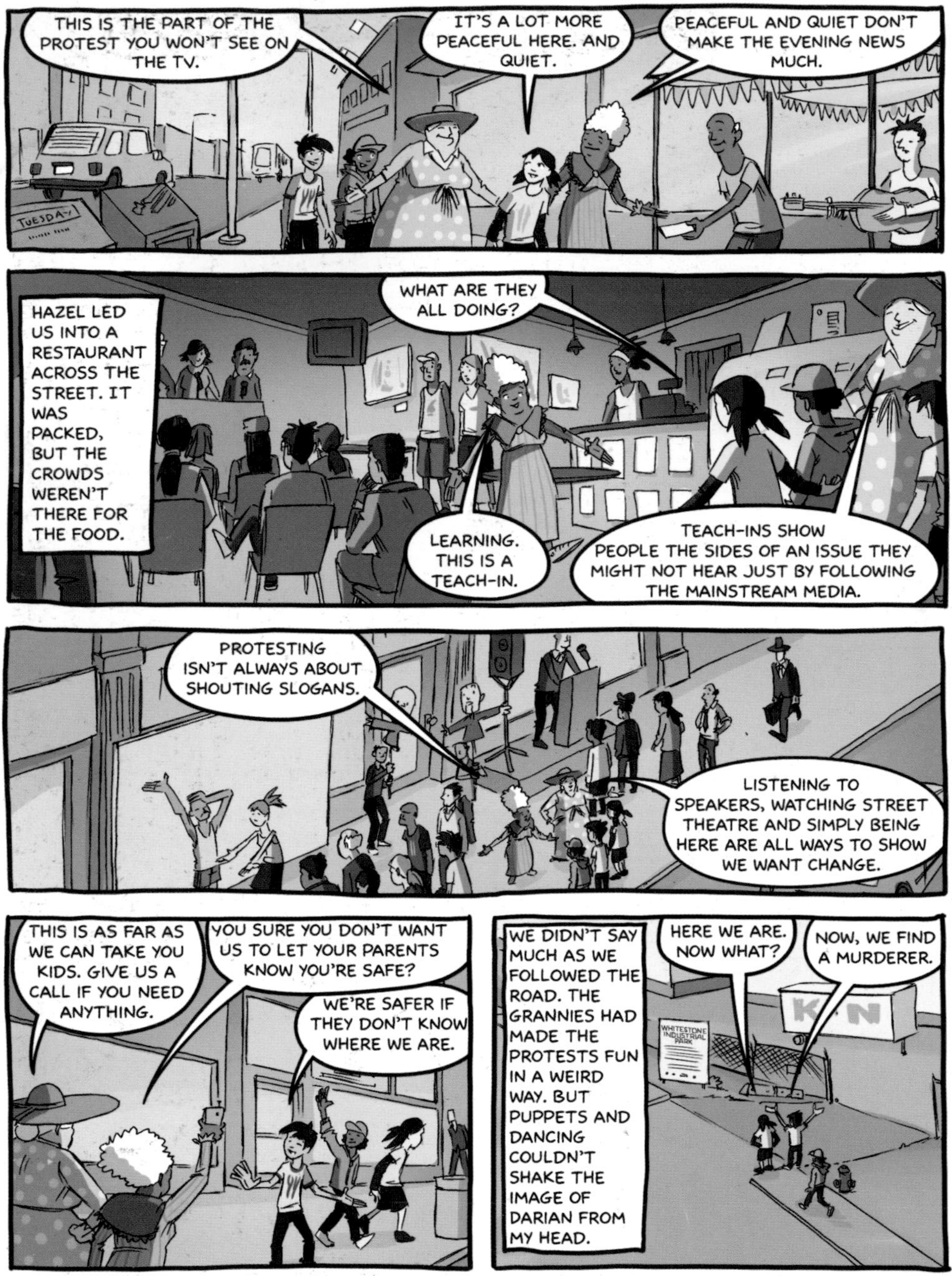

THIS IS THE PART OF THE PROTEST YOU WON'T SEE ON THE TV.
IT'S A LOT MORE PEACEFUL HERE. AND QUIET.
PEACEFUL AND QUIET DON'T MAKE THE EVENING NEWS MUCH.
HAZEL LED US INTO A RESTAURANT ACROSS THE STREET. IT WAS PACKED, BUT THE CROWDS WEREN'T THERE FOR THE FOOD.
WHAT ARE THEY ALL DOING?
LEARNING. THIS IS A TEACH-IN.
TEACH-INS SHOW PEOPLE THE SIDES OF AN ISSUE THEY MIGHT NOT HEAR JUST BY FOLLOWING THE MAINSTREAM MEDIA.
PROTESTING ISN'T ALWAYS ABOUT SHOUTING SLOGANS.
LISTENING TO SPEAKERS, WATCHING STREET THEATRE AND SIMPLY BEING HERE ARE ALL WAYS TO SHOW WE WANT CHANGE.
THIS IS AS FAR AS WE CAN TAKE YOU KIDS. GIVE US A CALL IF YOU NEED ANYTHING.
YOU SURE YOU DON'T WANT US TO LET YOUR PARENTS KNOW YOU'RE SAFE?
WE'RE SAFER IF THEY DON'T KNOW WHERE WE ARE.
WE DIDN'T SAY MUCH AS WE FOLLOWED THE ROAD. THE GRANNIES HAD MADE THE PROTESTS FUN IN A WEIRD WAY. BUT PUPPETS AND DANCING COULDN'T SHAKE THE IMAGE OF DARIAN FROM MY HEAD.
HERE WE ARE. NOW WHAT?
NOW, WE FIND A MURDERER.
WHITESTONE INDUSTRIAL PARK

CHAPTER 4
IN THE FLOW

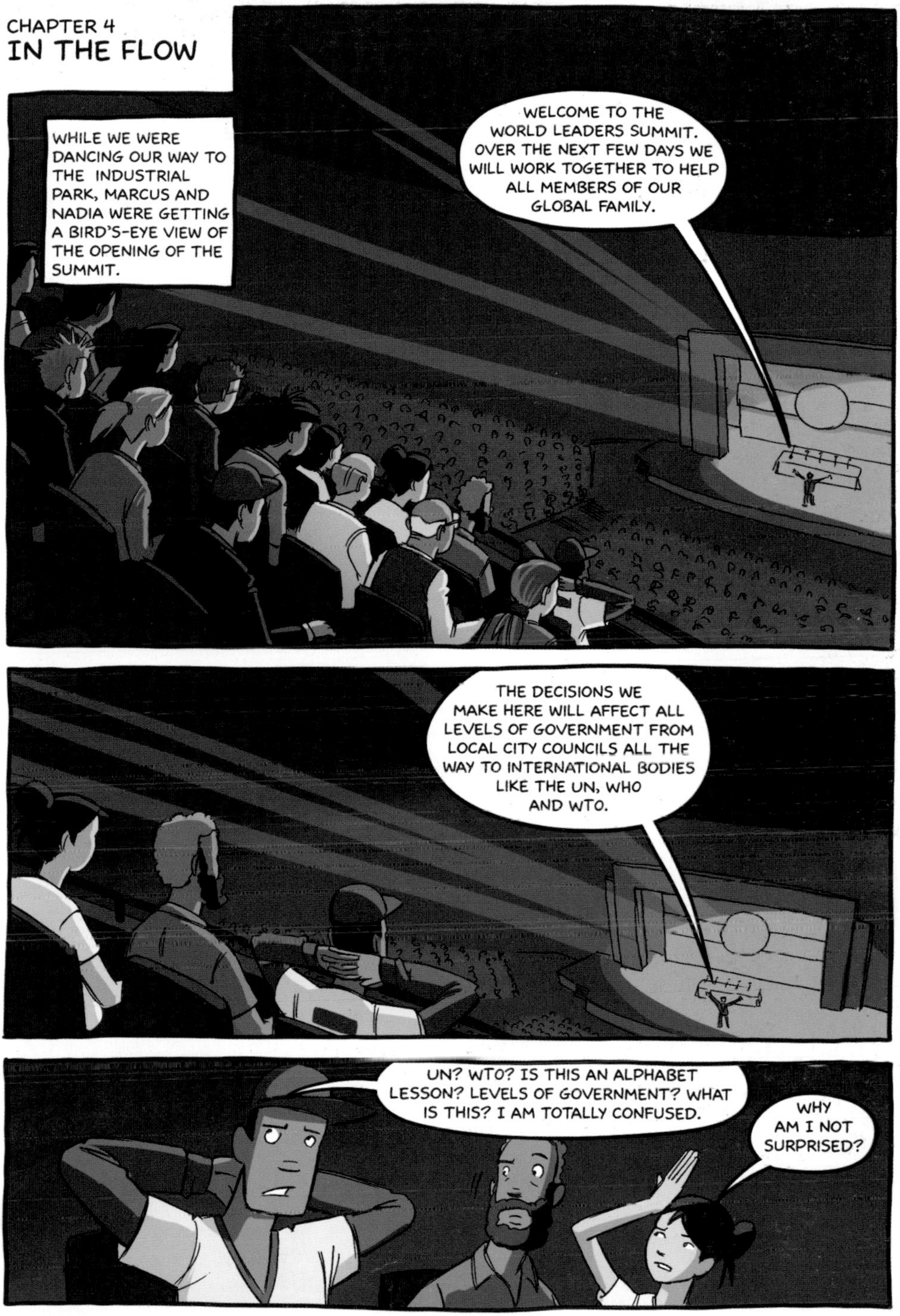
WHILE WE WERE DANCING OUR WAY TO THE INDUSTRIAL PARK, MARCUS AND NADIA WERE GETTING A BIRD'S-EYE VIEW OF THE OPENING OF THE SUMMIT.
WELCOME TO THE WORLD LEADERS SUMMIT. OVER THE NEXT FEW DAYS WE WILL WORK TOGETHER TO HELP ALL MEMBERS OF OUR GLOBAL FAMILY.
THE DECISIONS WE MAKE HERE WILL AFFECT ALL LEVELS OF GOVERNMENT FROM LOCAL CITY COUNCILS ALL THE WAY TO INTERNATIONAL BODIES LIKE THE UN, WHO AND WTO.
UN? WTO? IS THIS AN ALPHABET LESSON? LEVELS OF GOVERNMENT? WHAT IS THIS? I AM TOTALLY CONFUSED.
WHY AM I NOT SURPRISED?

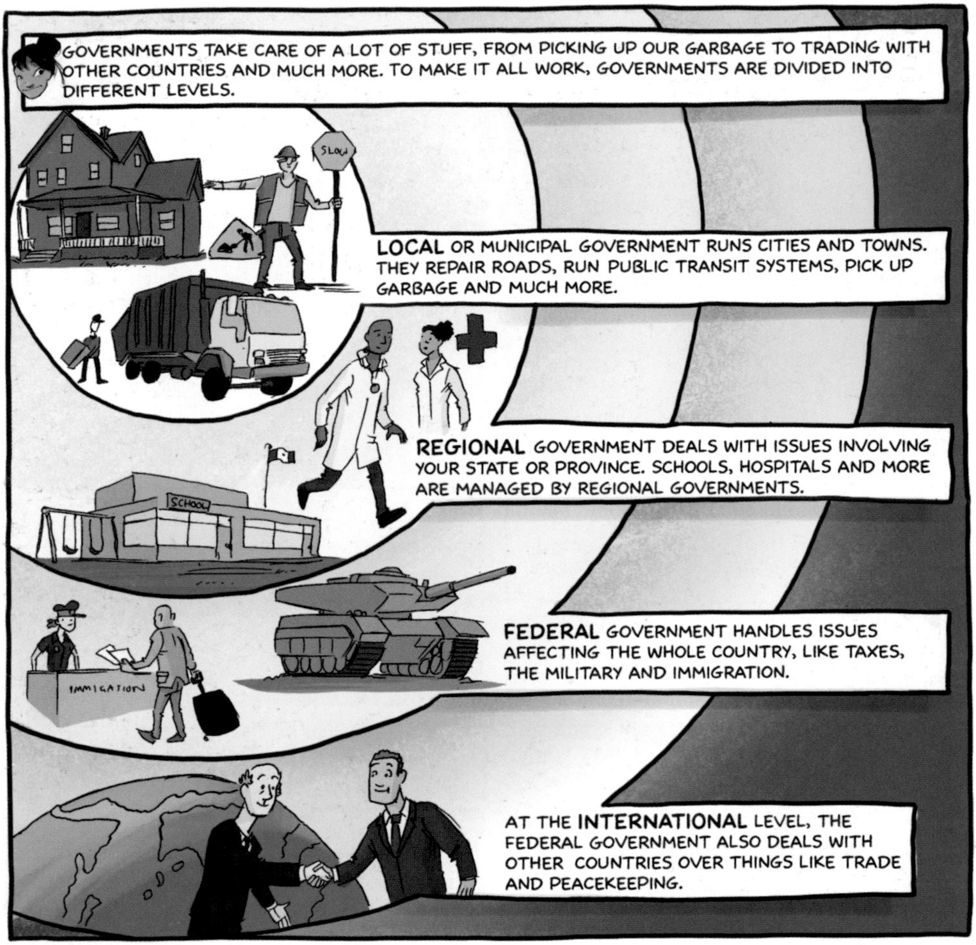
GOVERNMENTS TAKE CARE OF A LOT OF STUFF, FROM PICKING UP OUR GARBAGE TO TRADING WITH OTHER COUNTRIES AND MUCH MORE. TO MAKE IT ALL WORK, GOVERNMENTS ARE DIVIDED INTO DIFFERENT LEVELS.
SLOW
LOCAL OR MUNICIPAL GOVERNMENT RUNS CITIES AND TOWNS. THEY REPAIR ROADS, RUN PUBLIC TRANSIT SYSTEMS, PICK UP GARBAGE AND MUCH MORE.
REGIONAL GOVERNMENT DEALS WITH ISSUES INVOLVING YOUR STATE OR PROVINCE. SCHOOLS, HOSPITALS AND MORE ARE MANAGED BY REGIONAL GOVERNMENTS.
SCHOOL
IMMIGATION
FEDERAL GOVERNMENT HANDLES ISSUES AFFECTING THE WHOLE COUNTRY, LIKE TAXES, THE MILITARY AND IMMIGRATION.
AT THE INTERNATIONAL LEVEL, THE FEDERAL GOVERNMENT ALSO DEALS WITH OTHER COUNTRIES OVER THINGS LIKE TRADE AND PEACEKEEPING.

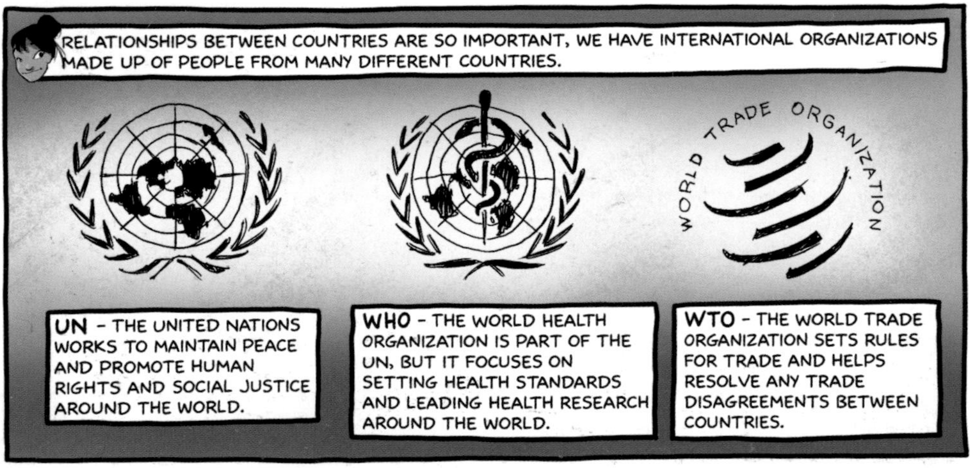
RELATIONSHIPS BETWEEN COUNTRIES ARE SO IMPORTANT, WE HAVE INTERNATIONAL ORGANIZATIONS MADE UP OF PEOPLE FROM MANY DIFFERENT COUNTRIES.
WORLD TRADE ORGANIZATION
UN – THE UNITED NATIONS WORKS TO MAINTAIN PEACE AND PROMOTE HUMAN RIGHTS AND SOCIAL JUSTICE AROUND THE WORLD.
WHO – THE WORLD HEALTH ORGANIZATION IS PART OF THE UN, BUT IT FOCUSES ON SETTING HEALTH STANDARDS AND LEADING HEALTH RESEARCH AROUND THE WORLD.
WTO – THE WORLD TRADE ORGANIZATION SETS RULES FOR TRADE AND HELPS RESOLVE ANY TRADE DISAGREEMENTS BETWEEN COUNTRIES.

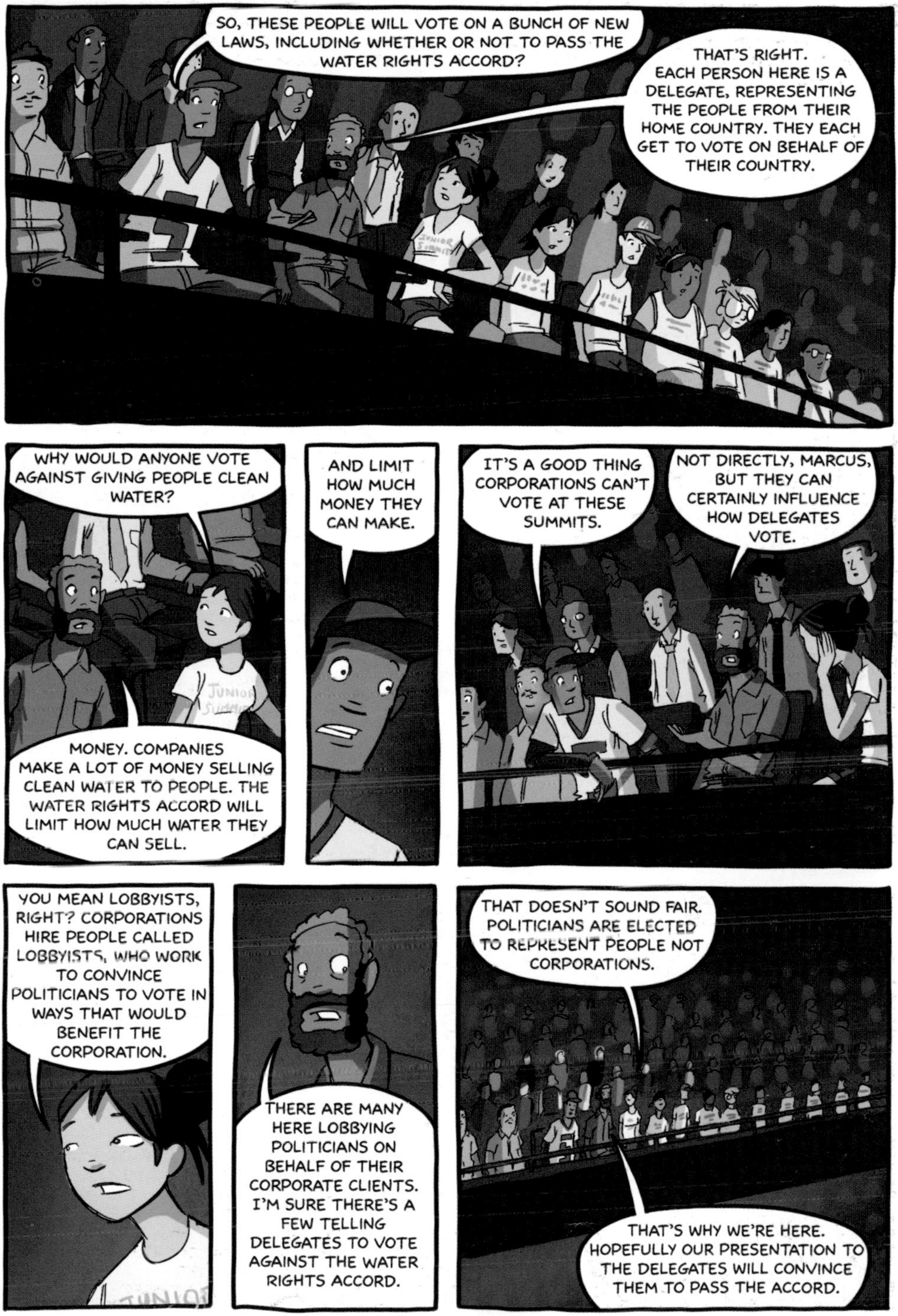
SO, THESE PEOPLE WILL VOTE ON A BUNCH OF NEW LAWS, INCLUDING WHETHER OR NOT TO PASS THE WATER RIGHTS ACCORD?
THAT'S RIGHT. EACH PERSON HERE IS A DELEGATE, REPRESENTING THE PEOPLE FROM THEIR HOME COUNTRY. THEY EACH GET TO VOTE ON BEHALF OF THEIR COUNTRY.
WHY WOULD ANYONE VOTE AGAINST GIVING PEOPLE CLEAN WATER?
MONEY. COMPANIES MAKE A LOT OF MONEY SELLING CLEAN WATER TO PEOPLE. THE WATER RIGHTS ACCORD WILL LIMIT HOW MUCH WATER THEY CAN SELL.
AND LIMIT HOW MUCH MONEY THEY CAN MAKE.
IT'S A GOOD THING CORPORATIONS CAN'T VOTE AT THESE SUMMITS.
NOT DIRECTLY, MARCUS, BUT THEY CAN CERTAINLY INFLUENCE HOW DELEGATES VOTE.
YOU MEAN LOBBYISTS, RIGHT? CORPORATIONS HIRE PEOPLE CALLED LOBBYISTS, WHO WORK TO CONVINCE POLITICIANS TO VOTE IN WAYS THAT WOULD BENEFIT THE CORPORATION.
THERE ARE MANY HERE LOBBYING POLITICIANS ON BEHALF OF THEIR CORPORATE CLIENTS. I'M SURE THERE'S A FEW TELLING DELEGATES TO VOTE AGAINST THE WATER RIGHTS ACCORD.
THAT DOESN'T SOUND FAIR. POLITICIANS ARE ELECTED TO REPRESENT PEOPLE NOT CORPORATIONS.
THAT'S WHY WE'RE HERE. HOPEFULLY OUR PRESENTATION TO THE DELEGATES WILL CONVINCE THEM TO PASS THE ACCORD.

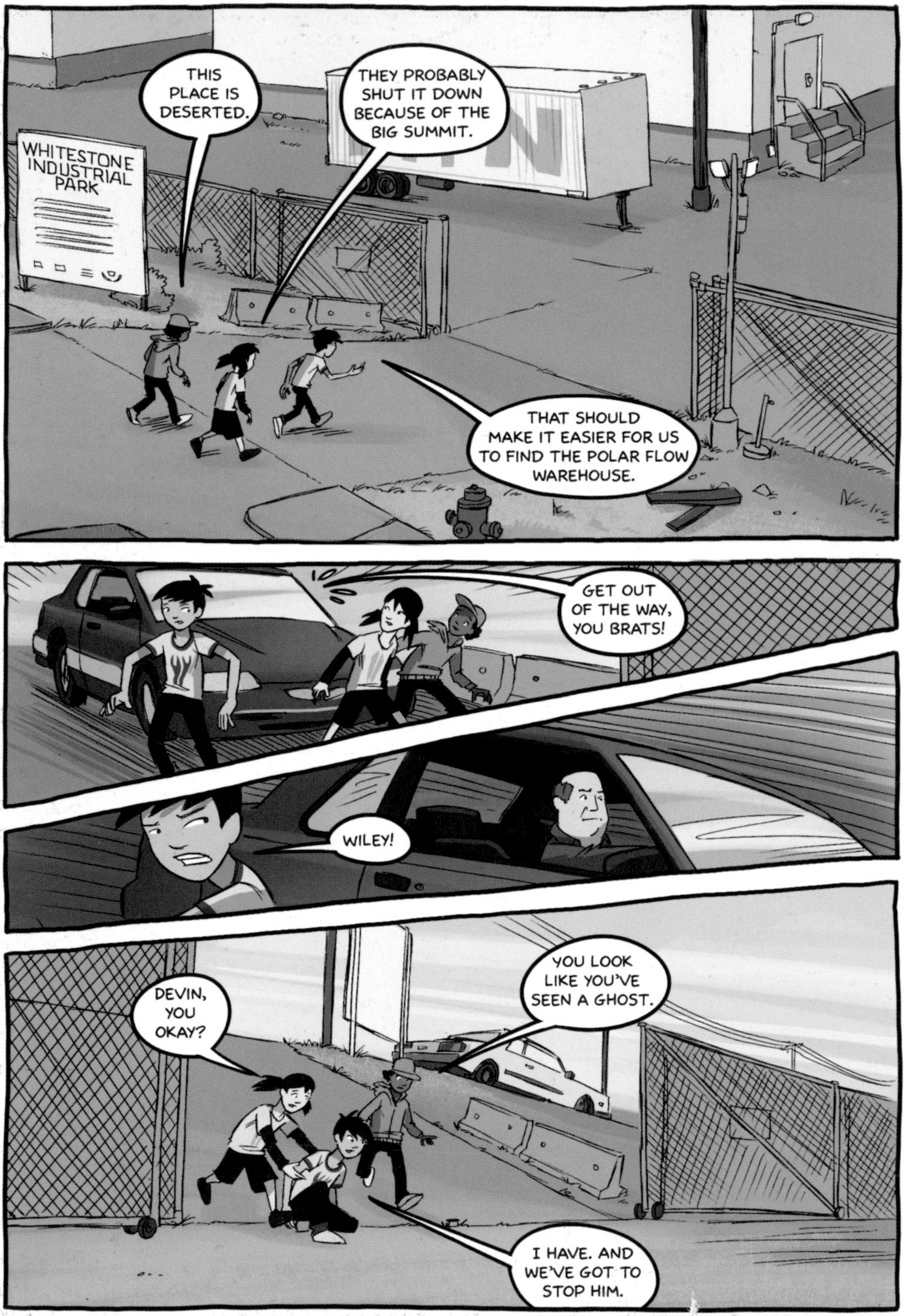
WHITESTONE INDUSTRIAL PARK
THIS PLACE IS DESERTED.
THEY PROBABLY SHUT IT DOWN BECAUSE OF THE BIG SUMMIT.
THAT SHOULD MAKE IT EASIER FOR US TO FIND THE POLAR FLOW WAREHOUSE.
GET OUT OF THE WAY, YOU BRATS!
WILEY!
DEVIN, YOU OKAY?
YOU LOOK LIKE YOU'VE SEEN A GHOST.
I HAVE. AND WE'VE GOT TO STOP HIM.

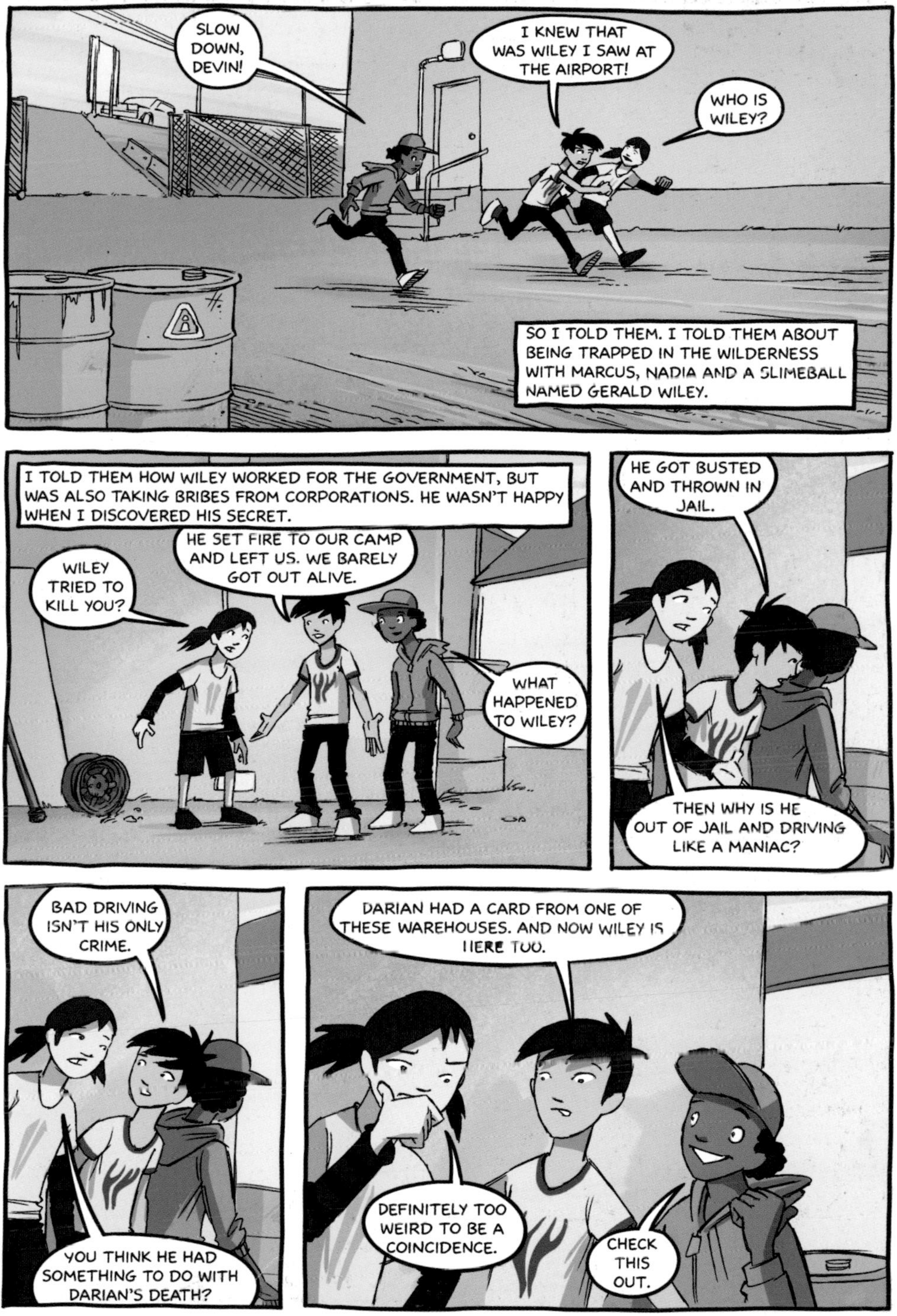
SLOW DOWN, DEVIN!
I KNEW THAT WAS WILEY I SAW AT THE AIRPORT!
WHO IS WILEY?
SO I TOLD THEM. I TOLD THEM ABOUT BEING TRAPPED IN THE WILDERNESS WITH MARCUS, NADIA AND A SLIMEBALL NAMED GERALD WILEY.
I TOLD THEM HOW WILEY WORKED FOR THE GOVERNMENT, BUT WAS ALSO TAKING BRIBES FROM CORPORATIONS. HE WASN'T HAPPY WHEN I DISCOVERED HIS SECRET.
WILEY TRIED TO KILL YOU?
HE SET FIRE TO OUR CAMP AND LEFT US. WE BARELY GOT OUT ALIVE.
WHAT HAPPENED TO WILEY?
HE GOT BUSTED AND THROWN IN JAIL.
THEN WHY IS HE OUT OF JAIL AND DRIVING LIKE A MANIAC?
BAD DRIVING ISN'T HIS ONLY CRIME.
YOU THINK HE HAD SOMETHING TO DO WITH DARIAN'S DEATH?
DARIAN HAD A CARD FROM ONE OF THESE WAREHOUSES. AND NOW WILEY IS HERE TOO.
DEFINITELY TOO WEIRD TO BE A COINCIDENCE.
CHECK THIS OUT.

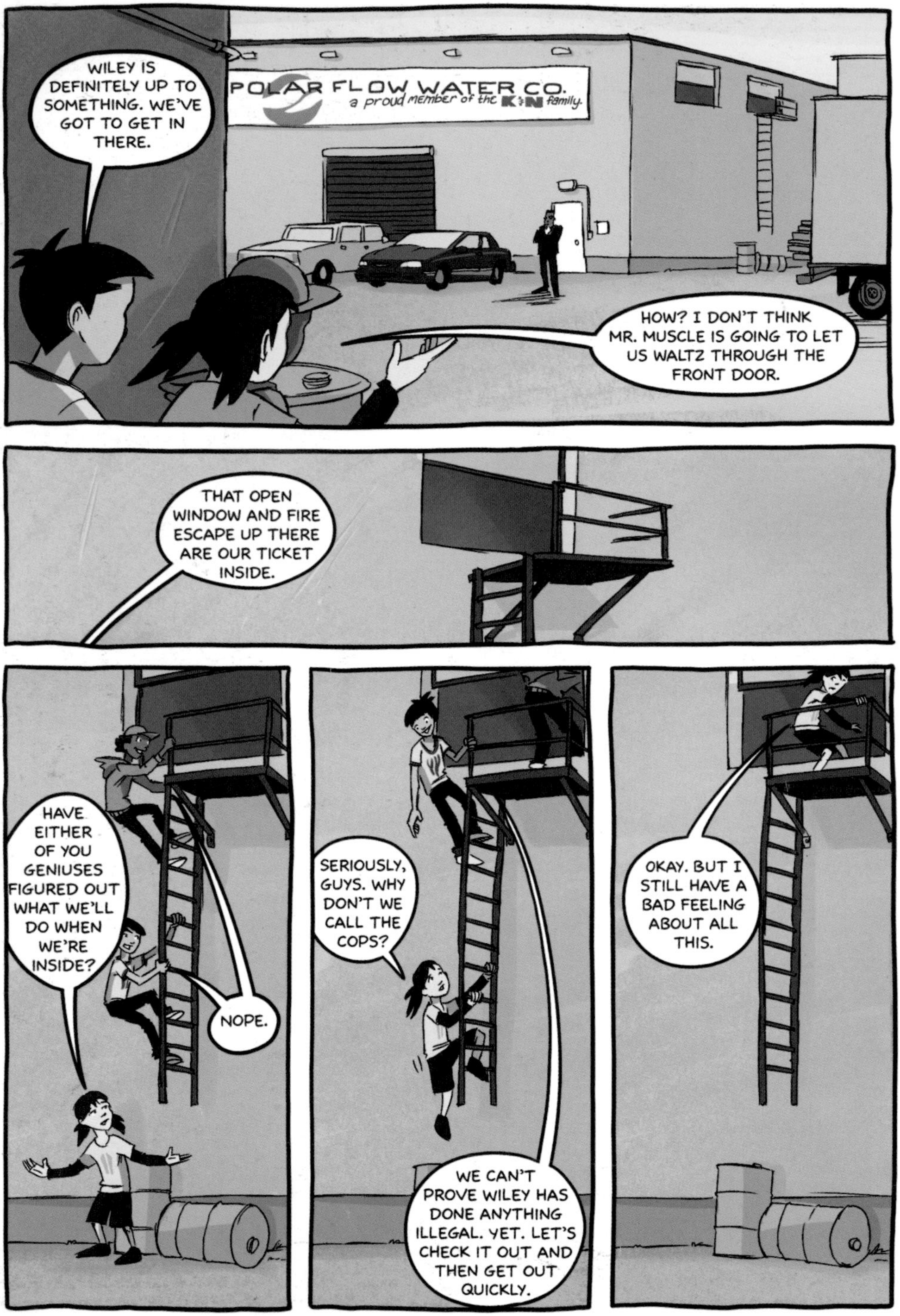
WILEY IS DEFINITELY UP TO SOMETHING. WE'VE GOT TO GET IN THERE.
POLAR FLOW WATER CO.
a proud member of the K N family.
HOW? I DON'T THINK MR. MUSCLE IS GOING TO LET US WALTZ THROUGH THE FRONT DOOR.
THAT OPEN WINDOW AND FIRE ESCAPE UP THERE ARE OUR TICKET INSIDE.
HAVE EITHER OF YOU GENIUSES FIGURED OUT WHAT WE'LL DO WHEN WE'RE INSIDE?
NOPE.
SERIOUSLY, GUYS. WHY DON'T WE CALL THE COPS?
WE CAN'T PROVE WILEY HAS DONE ANYTHING ILLEGAL. YET. LET'S CHECK IT OUT AND THEN GET OUT QUICKLY.
OKAY. BUT I STILL HAVE A BAD FEELING ABOUT ALL THIS.

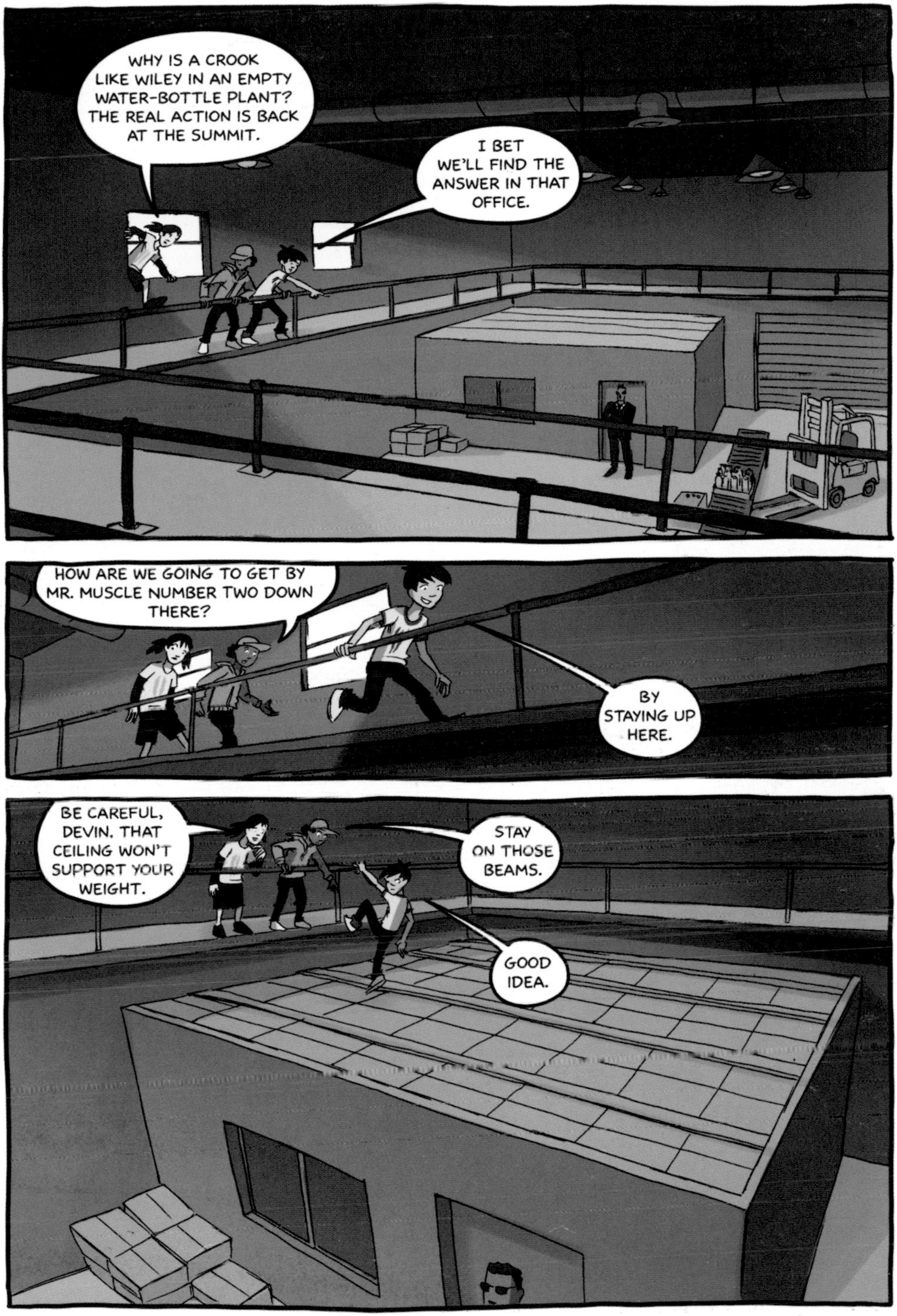
WHY IS A CROOK LIKE WILEY IN AN EMPTY WATER-BOTTLE PLANT? THE REAL ACTION IS BACK AT THE SUMMIT.
I BET WE'LL FIND THE ANSWER IN THAT OFFICE.
HOW ARE WE GOING TO GET BY MR. MUSCLE NUMBER TWO DOWN THERE?
BY STAYING UP HERE.
BE CAREFUL, DEVIN. THAT CEILING WON'T SUPPORT YOUR WEIGHT.
STAY ON THOSE BEAMS.
GOOD IDEA.

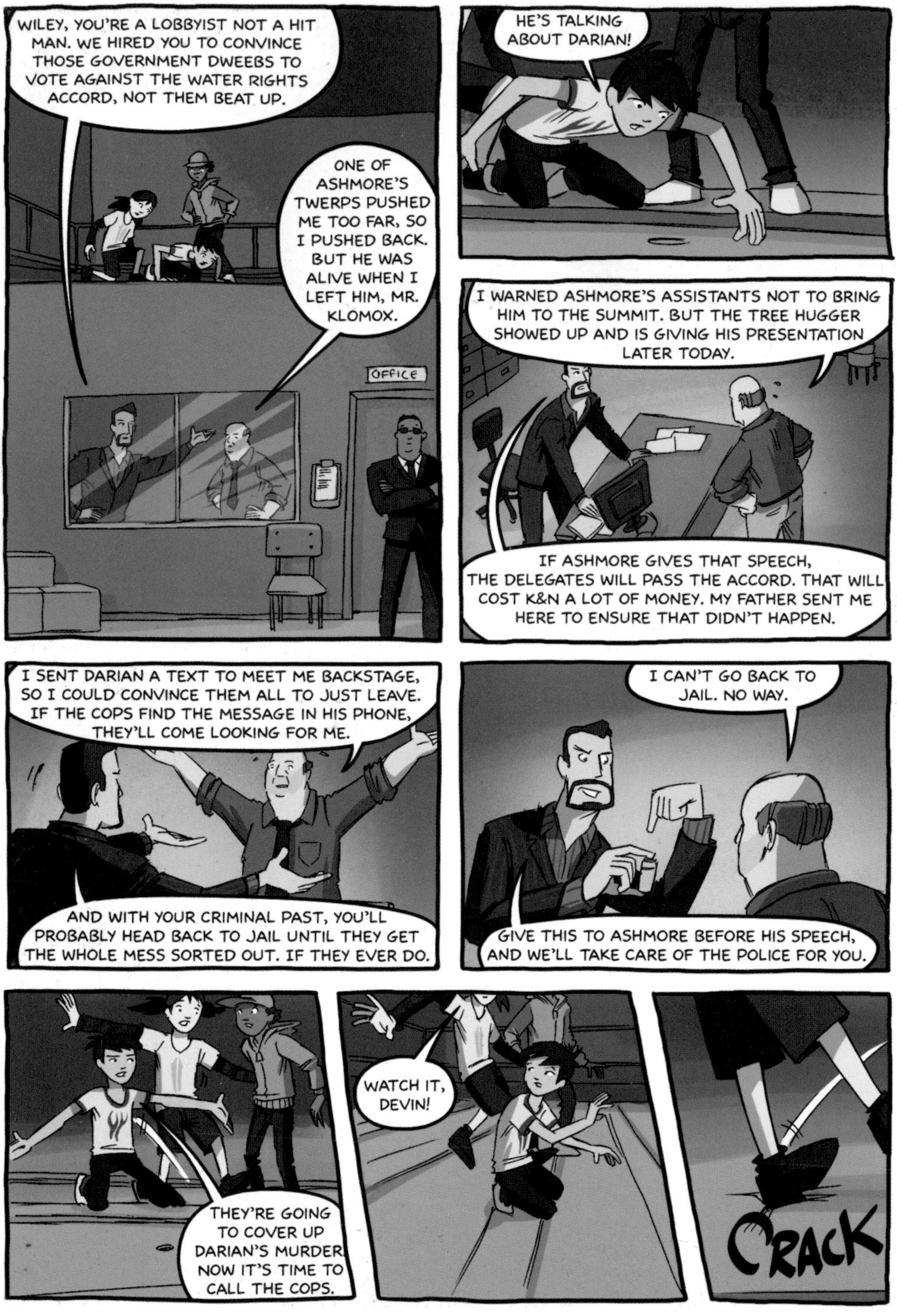
WILEY, YOU'RE A LOBBYIST NOT A HIT MAN. WE HIRED YOU TO CONVINCE THOSE GOVERNMENT DWEEBS TO VOTE AGAINST THE WATER RIGHTS ACCORD, NOT THEM BEAT UP.
ONE OF ASHMORE'S TWERPS PUSHED ME TOO FAR, SO I PUSHED BACK. BUT HE WAS ALIVE WHEN I LEFT HIM, MR. KLOMOX.
OFFICE
HE'S TALKING ABOUT DARIAN!
I WARNED ASHMORE'S ASSISTANTS NOT TO BRING HIM TO THE SUMMIT. BUT THE TREE HUGGER SHOWED UP AND IS GIVING HIS PRESENTATION LATER TODAY.
IF ASHMORE GIVES THAT SPEECH, THE DELEGATES WILL PASS THE ACCORD. THAT WILL COST K&N A LOT OF MONEY. MY FATHER SENT ME HERE TO ENSURE THAT DIDN'T HAPPEN.
I SENT DARIAN A TEXT TO MEET ME BACKSTAGE, SO I COULD CONVINCE THEM ALL TO JUST LEAVE. IF THE COPS FIND THE MESSAGE IN HIS PHONE, THEY'LL COME LOOKING FOR ME.
AND WITH YOUR CRIMINAL PAST, YOU'LL PROBABLY HEAD BACK TO JAIL UNTIL THEY GET THE WHOLE MESS SORTED OUT. IF THEY EVER DO.
I CAN'T GO BACK TO JAIL. NO WAY.
GIVE THIS TO ASHMORE BEFORE HIS SPEECH, AND WE'LL TAKE CARE OF THE POLICE FOR YOU.
THEY'RE GOING TO COVER UP DARIAN'S MURDER. NOW IT'S TIME TO CALL THE COPS.
WATCH IT, DEVIN!
CRACK

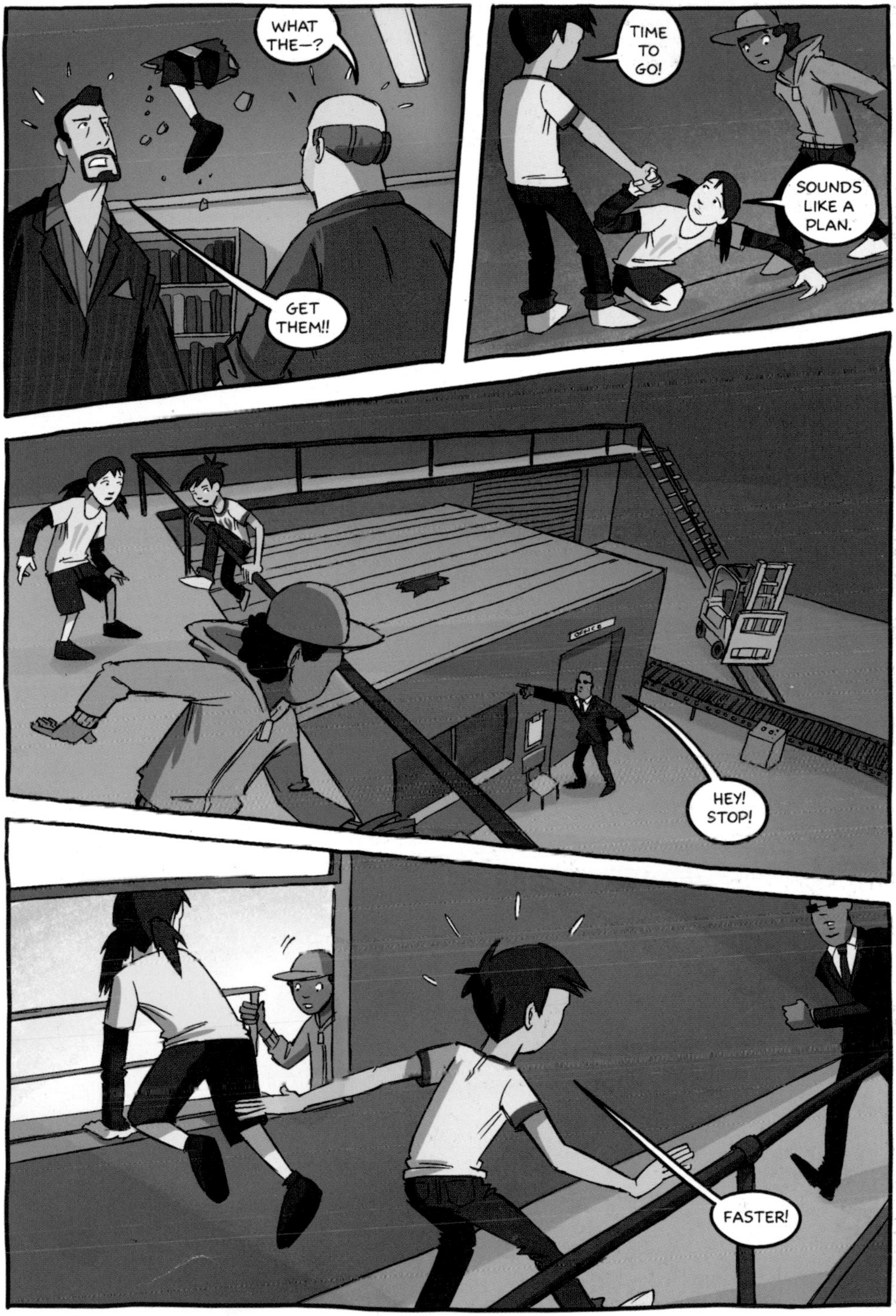

WHAT THE—?
GET THEM!!
TIME TO GO!
SOUNDS LIKE A PLAN.
HEY! STOP!
FASTER!

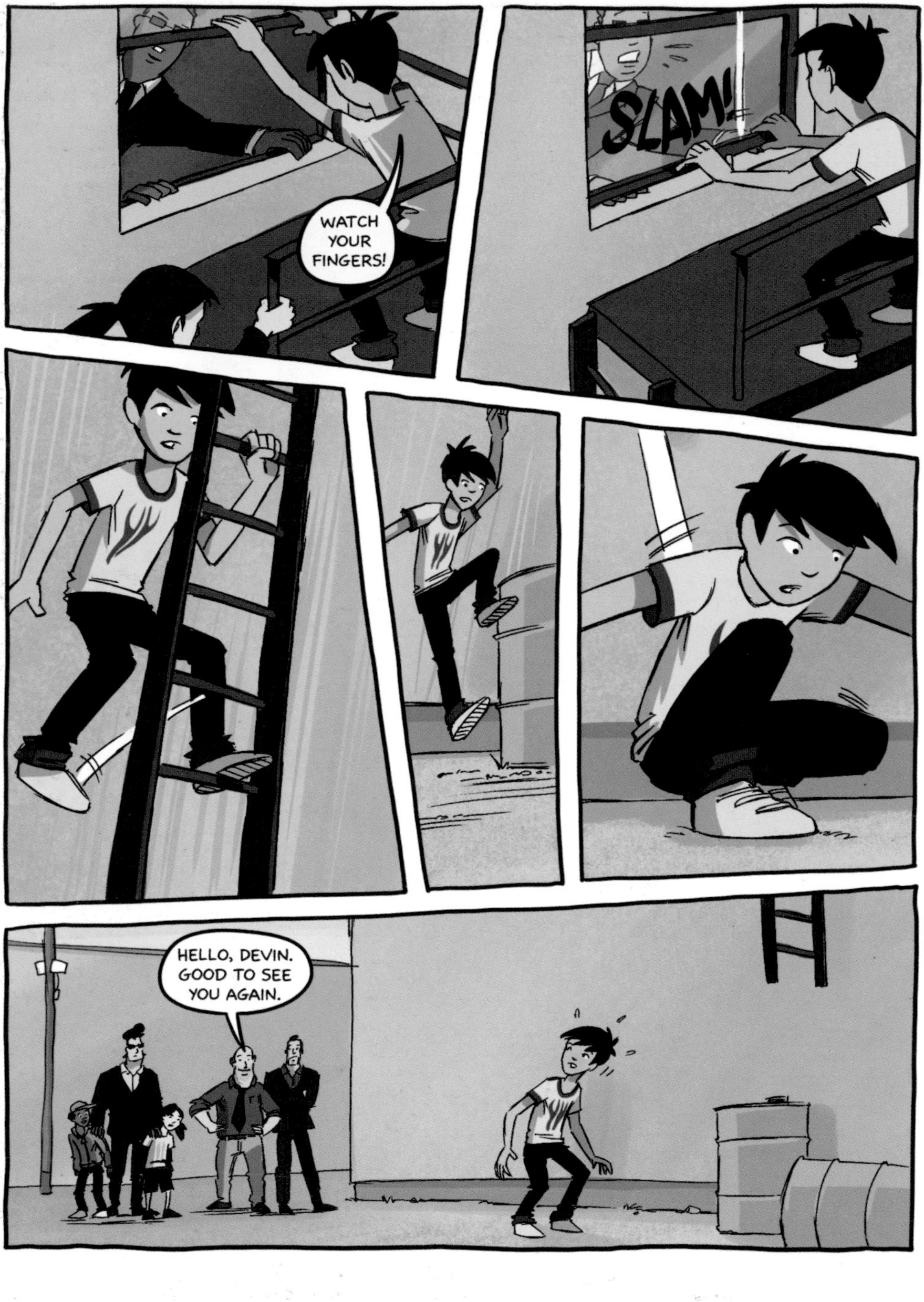
WATCH YOUR FINGERS!
SLAM!
HELLO, DEVIN. GOOD TO SEE YOU AGAIN.

CHAPTER 5
BURGERS AND BACKROOM DEALS

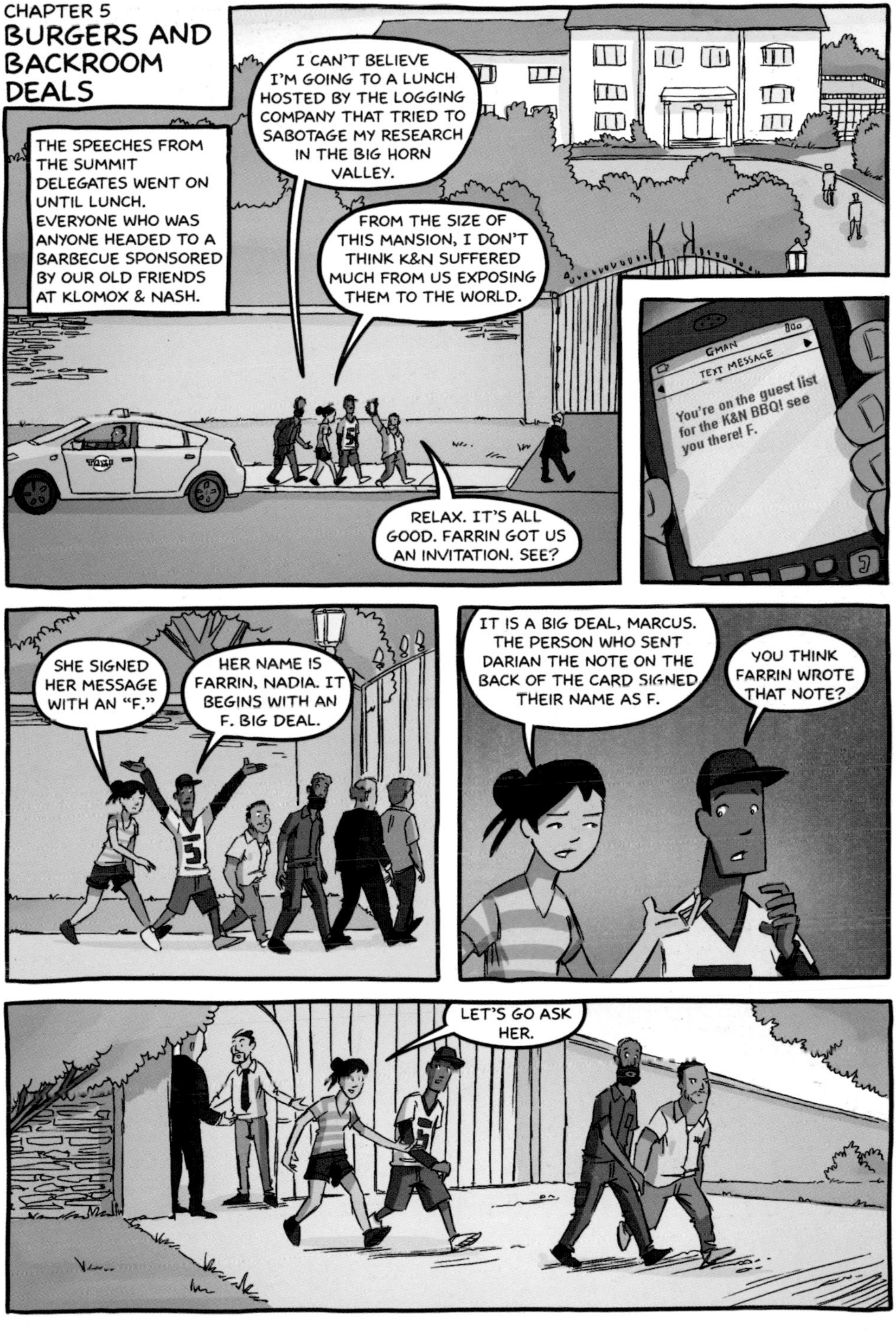
THE SPEECHES FROM THE SUMMIT DELEGATES WENT ON UNTIL LUNCH. EVERYONE WHO WAS ANYONE HEADED TO A BARBECUE SPONSORED BY OUR OLD FRIENDS AT KLOMOX & NASH.
I CAN'T BELIEVE I'M GOING TO A LUNCH HOSTED BY THE LOGGING COMPANY THAT TRIED TO SABOTAGE MY RESEARCH IN THE BIG HORN VALLEY.
FROM THE SIZE OF THIS MANSION, I DON'T THINK K&N SUFFERED MUCH FROM US EXPOSING THEM TO THE WORLD.
RELAX. IT'S ALL GOOD. FARRIN GOT US AN INVITATION. SEE?
GMAN
TEXT MESSAGE
You're on the guest list for the K&N BBQ! see you there! F.
SHE SIGNED HER MESSAGE WITH AN "F."
HER NAME IS FARRIN, NADIA. IT BEGINS WITH AN F. BIG DEAL.
IT IS A BIG DEAL, MARCUS. THE PERSON WHO SENT DARIAN THE NOTE ON THE BACK OF THE CARD SIGNED THEIR NAME AS F.
YOU THINK FARRIN WROTE THAT NOTE?
LET'S GO ASK HER.

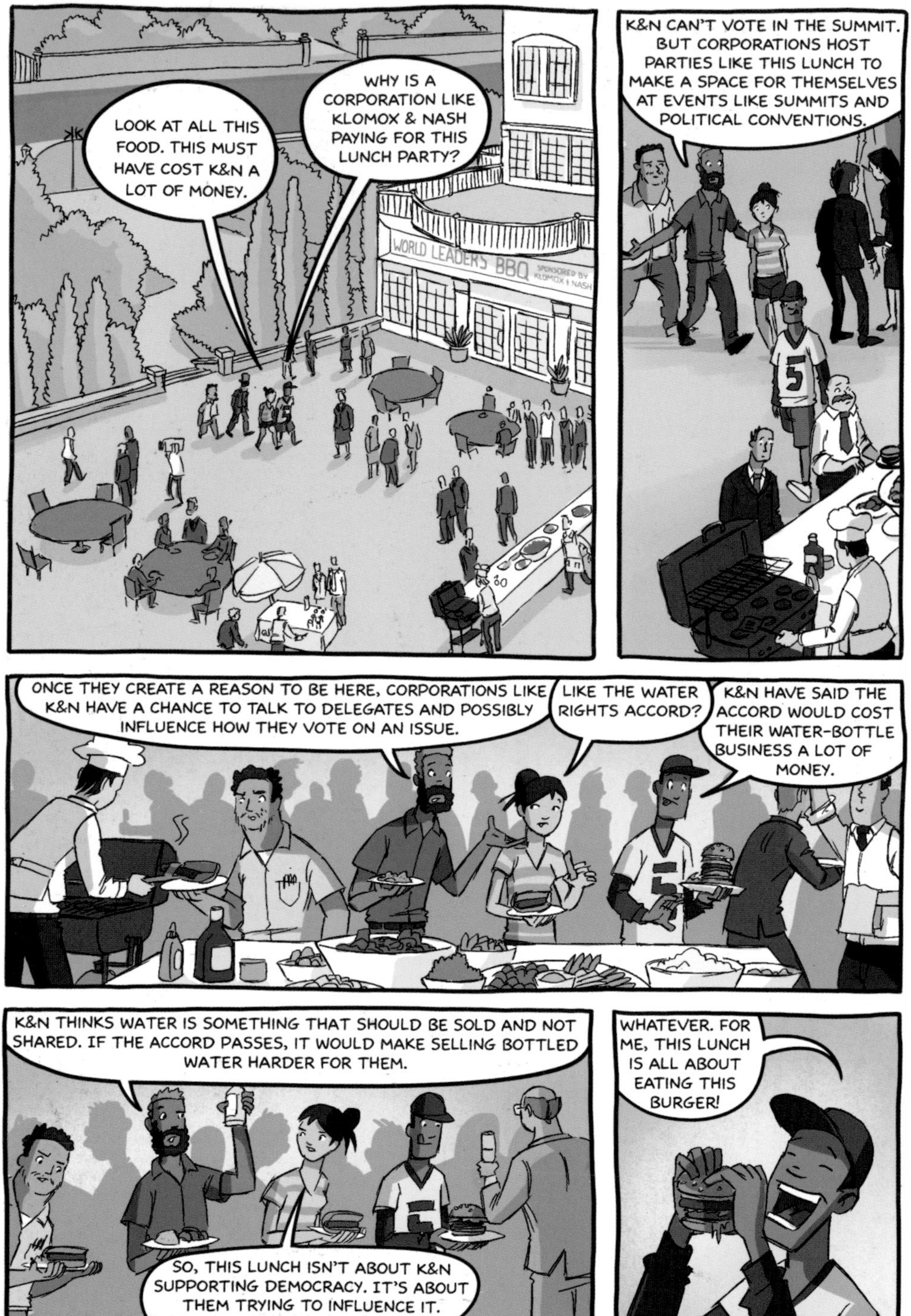
LOOK AT ALL THIS FOOD. THIS MUST HAVE COST K&N A LOT OF MONEY.
WHY IS A CORPORATION LIKE KLOMOX & NASH PAYING FOR THIS LUNCH PARTY?
WORLD LEADERS BBQ
SPONSORED BY KLOMOX & NASH
K&N CAN'T VOTE IN THE SUMMIT. BUT CORPORATIONS HOST PARTIES LIKE THIS LUNCH TO MAKE A SPACE FOR THEMSELVES AT EVENTS LIKE SUMMITS AND POLITICAL CONVENTIONS.
ONCE THEY CREATE A REASON TO BE HERE, CORPORATIONS LIKE K&N HAVE A CHANCE TO TALK TO DELEGATES AND POSSIBLY INFLUENCE HOW THEY VOTE ON AN ISSUE.
LIKE THE WATER RIGHTS ACCORD?
K&N HAVE SAID THE ACCORD WOULD COST THEIR WATER-BOTTLE BUSINESS A LOT OF MONEY.
K&N THINKS WATER IS SOMETHING THAT SHOULD BE SOLD AND NOT SHARED. IF THE ACCORD PASSES, IT WOULD MAKE SELLING BOTTLED WATER HARDER FOR THEM.
SO, THIS LUNCH ISN'T ABOUT K&N SUPPORTING DEMOCRACY. IT'S ABOUT THEM TRYING TO INFLUENCE IT.
WHATEVER. FOR ME, THIS LUNCH IS ALL ABOUT EATING THIS BURGER!

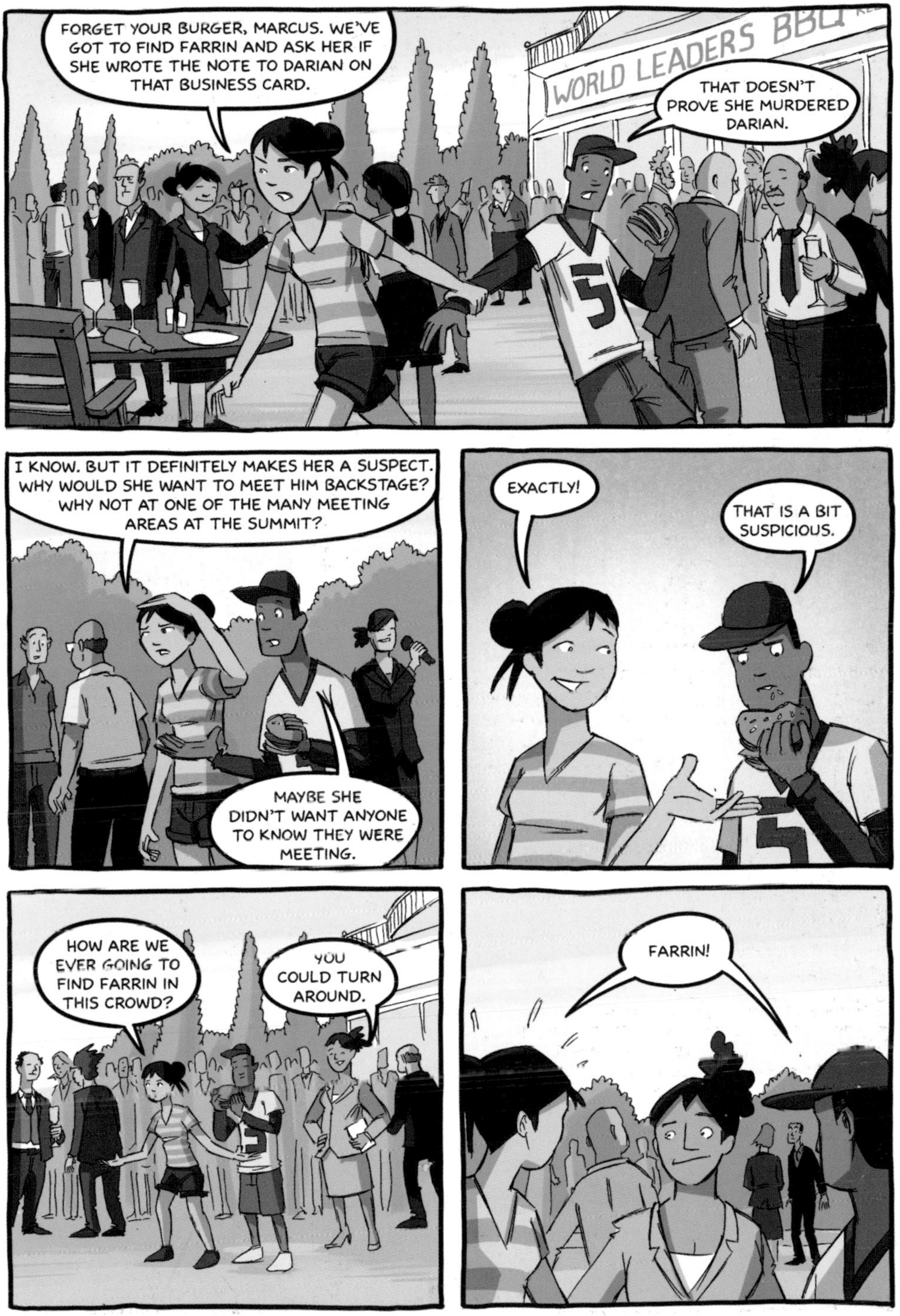
FORGET YOUR BURGER, MARCUS. WE'VE GOT TO FIND FARRIN AND ASK HER IF SHE WROTE THE NOTE TO DARIAN ON THAT BUSINESS CARD.
WORLD LEADERS BBQ
THAT DOESN'T PROVE SHE MURDERED DARIAN.
I KNOW. BUT IT DEFINITELY MAKES HER A SUSPECT. WHY WOULD SHE WANT TO MEET HIM BACKSTAGE? WHY NOT AT ONE OF THE MANY MEETING AREAS AT THE SUMMIT?
MAYBE SHE DIDN'T WANT ANYONE TO KNOW THEY WERE MEETING.
EXACTLY!
THAT IS A BIT SUSPICIOUS.
HOW ARE WE EVER GOING TO FIND FARRIN IN THIS CROWD?
YOU COULD TURN AROUND.
FARRIN!

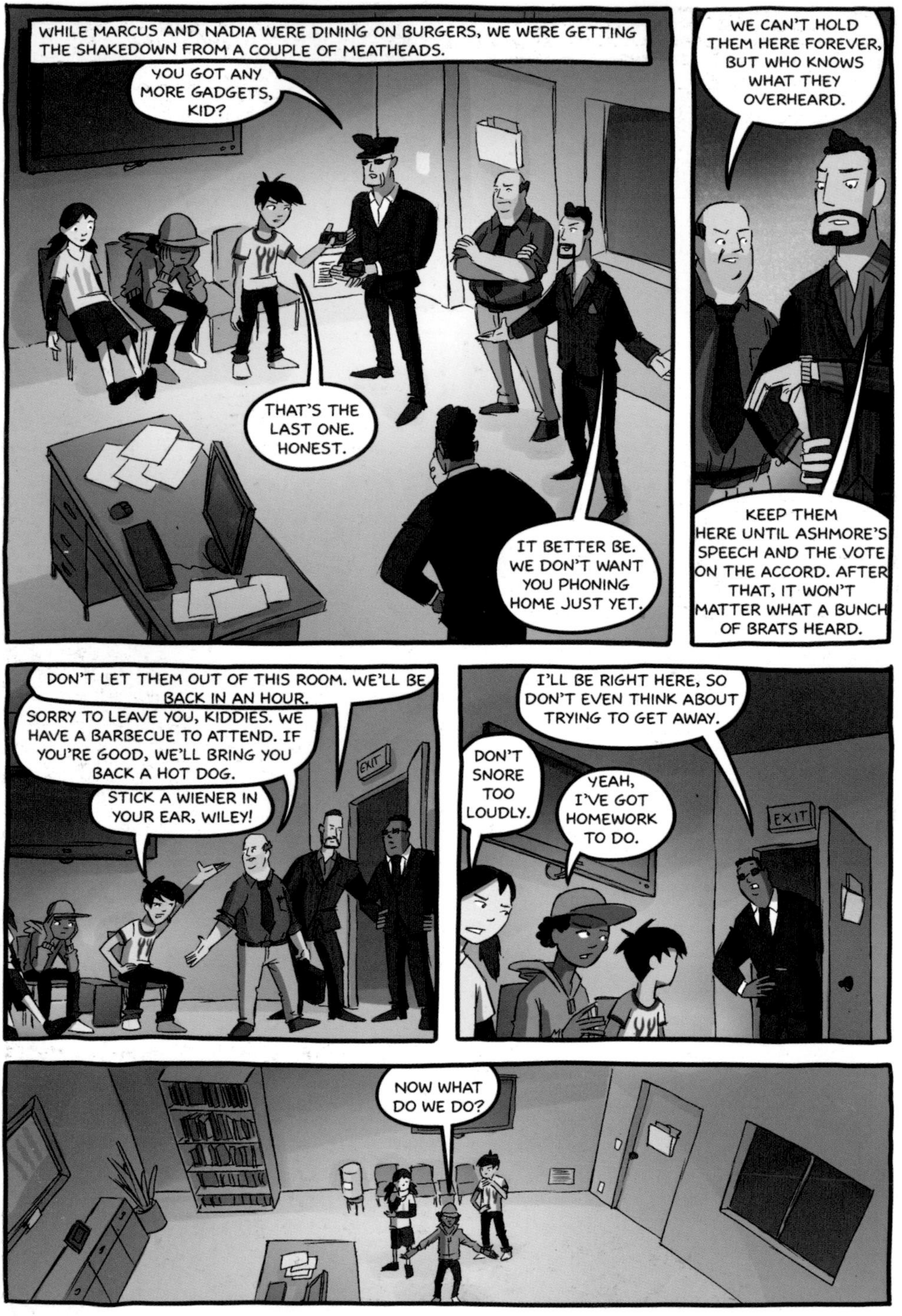
WHILE MARCUS AND NADIA WERE DINING ON BURGERS, WE WERE GETTING THE SHAKEDOWN FROM A COUPLE OF MEATHEADS.
YOU GOT ANY MORE GADGETS, KID?
THAT'S THE LAST ONE. HONEST.
IT BETTER BE. WE DON'T WANT YOU PHONING HOME JUST YET.
WE CAN'T HOLD THEM HERE FOREVER, BUT WHO KNOWS WHAT THEY OVERHEARD.
KEEP THEM HERE UNTIL ASHMORE'S SPEECH AND THE VOTE ON THE ACCORD. AFTER THAT, IT WON'T MATTER WHAT A BUNCH OF BRATS HEARD.
DON'T LET THEM OUT OF THIS ROOM. WE'LL BE BACK IN AN HOUR.
SORRY TO LEAVE YOU, KIDDIES. WE HAVE A BARBECUE TO ATTEND. IF YOU'RE GOOD, WE'LL BRING YOU BACK A HOT DOG.
STICK A WIENER IN YOUR EAR, WILEY!
EXIT
I'LL BE RIGHT HERE, SO DON'T EVEN THINK ABOUT TRYING TO GET AWAY.
DON'T SNORE TOO LOUDLY.
YEAH, I'VE GOT HOMEWORK TO DO.
EXIT
NOW WHAT DO WE DO?

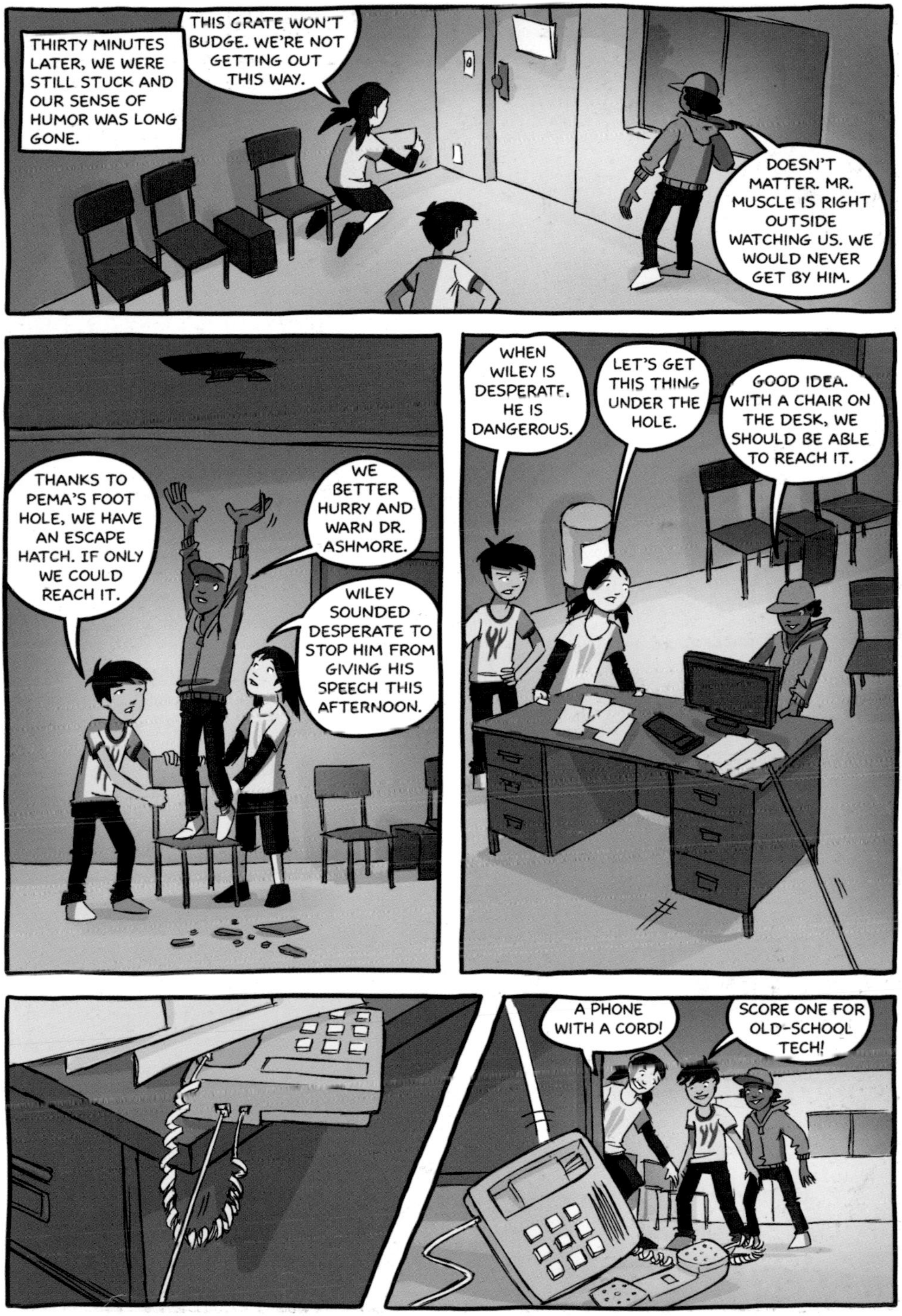
THIRTY MINUTES LATER, WE WERE STILL STUCK AND OUR SENSE OF HUMOR WAS LONG GONE.
THIS GRATE WON'T BUDGE. WE'RE NOT GETTING OUT THIS WAY.
DOESN'T MATTER. MR. MUSCLE IS RIGHT OUTSIDE WATCHING US. WE WOULD NEVER GET BY HIM.
THANKS TO PEMA'S FOOT HOLE, WE HAVE AN ESCAPE HATCH. IF ONLY WE COULD REACH IT.
WE BETTER HURRY AND WARN DR. ASHMORE.
WILEY SOUNDED DESPERATE TO STOP HIM FROM GIVING HIS SPEECH THIS AFTERNOON.
WHEN WILEY IS DESPERATE, HE IS DANGEROUS.
LET'S GET THIS THING UNDER THE HOLE.
GOOD IDEA. WITH A CHAIR ON THE DESK, WE SHOULD BE ABLE TO REACH IT.
A PHONE WITH A CORD!
SCORE ONE FOR OLD-SCHOOL TECH!

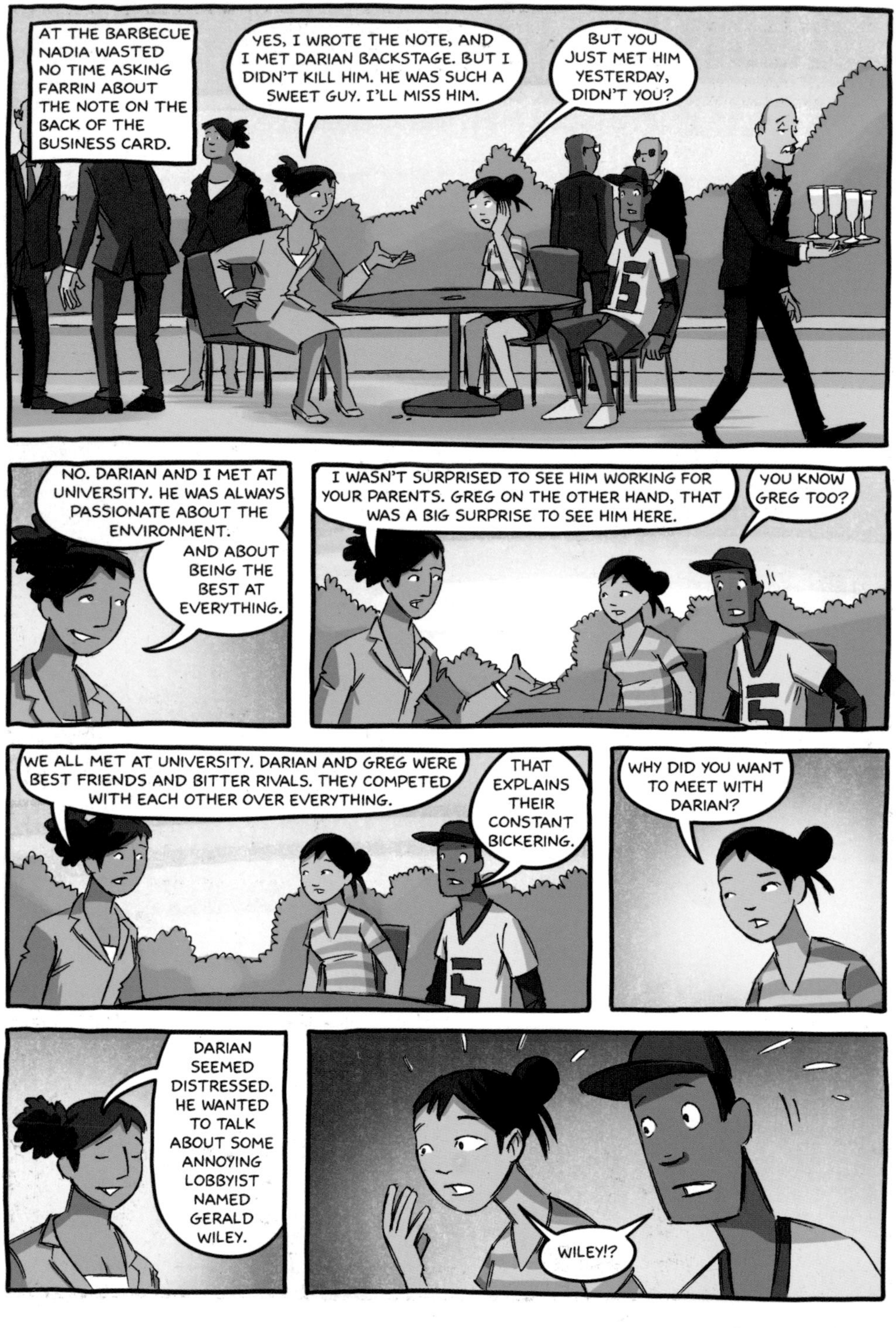
AT THE BARBECUE NADIA WASTED NO TIME ASKING FARRIN ABOUT THE NOTE ON THE BACK OF THE BUSINESS CARD.
YES, I WROTE THE NOTE, AND I MET DARIAN BACKSTAGE. BUT I DIDN'T KILL HIM. HE WAS SUCH A SWEET GUY. I'LL MISS HIM.
BUT YOU JUST MET HIM YESTERDAY, DIDN'T YOU?
NO. DARIAN AND I MET AT UNIVERSITY. HE WAS ALWAYS PASSIONATE ABOUT THE ENVIRONMENT.
AND ABOUT BEING THE BEST AT EVERYTHING.
I WASN'T SURPRISED TO SEE HIM WORKING FOR YOUR PARENTS. GREG ON THE OTHER HAND, THAT WAS A BIG SURPRISE TO SEE HIM HERE.
YOU KNOW GREG TOO?
WE ALL MET AT UNIVERSITY. DARIAN AND GREG WERE BEST FRIENDS AND BITTER RIVALS. THEY COMPETED WITH EACH OTHER OVER EVERYTHING.
THAT EXPLAINS THEIR CONSTANT BICKERING.
WHY DID YOU WANT TO MEET WITH DARIAN?
DARIAN SEEMED DISTRESSED. HE WANTED TO TALK ABOUT SOME ANNOYING LOBBYIST NAMED GERALD WILEY.
WILEY!?

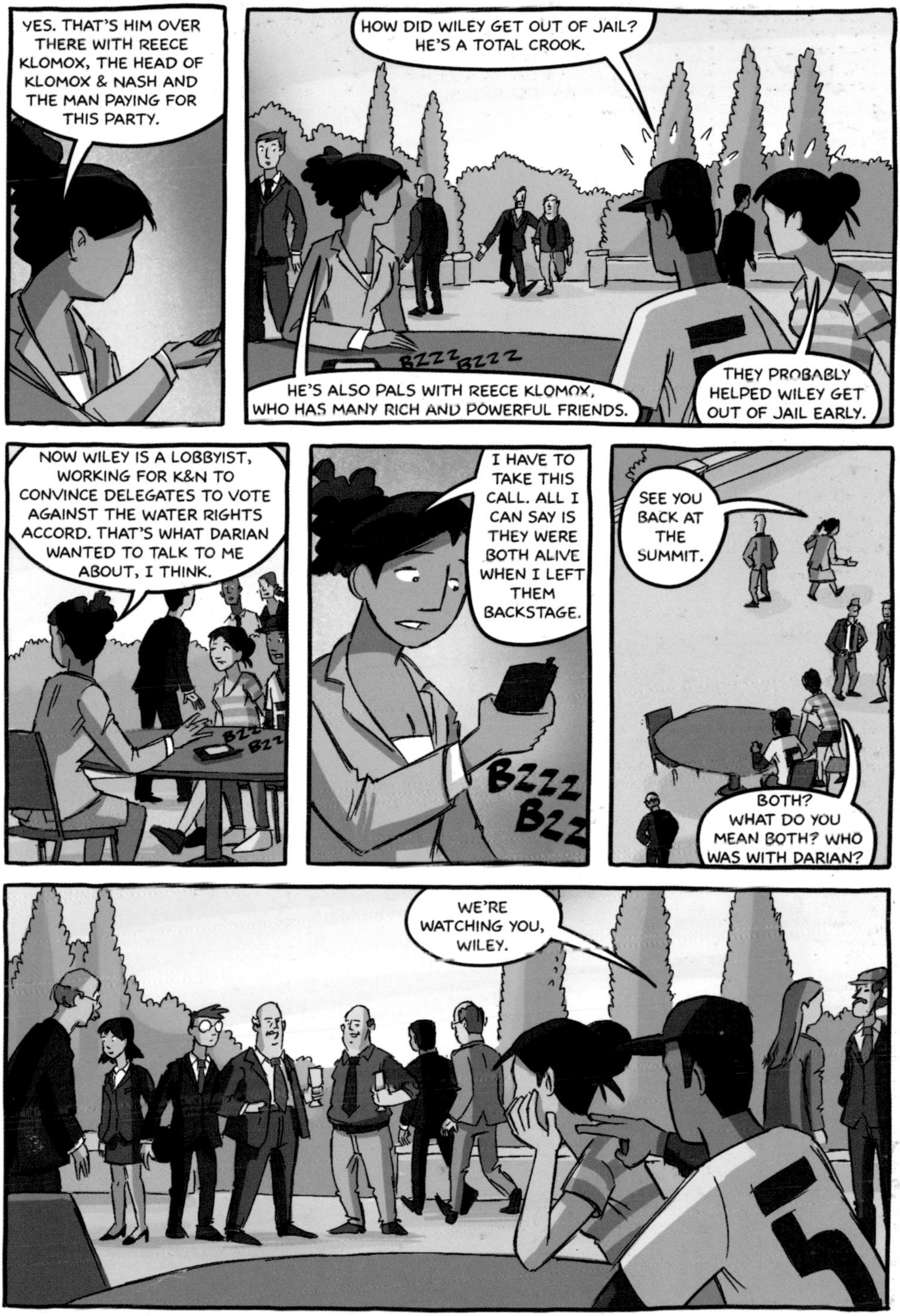
YES. THAT'S HIM OVER THERE WITH REECE KLOMOX, THE HEAD OF KLOMOX & NASH AND THE MAN PAYING FOR THIS PARTY.
HOW DID WILEY GET OUT OF JAIL? HE'S A TOTAL CROOK.
BZZZ BZZZ
HE'S ALSO PALS WITH REECE KLOMOX, WHO HAS MANY RICH AND POWERFUL FRIENDS.
THEY PROBABLY HELPED WILEY GET OUT OF JAIL EARLY.
NOW WILEY IS A LOBBYIST, WORKING FOR K&N TO CONVINCE DELEGATES TO VOTE AGAINST THE WATER RIGHTS ACCORD. THAT'S WHAT DARIAN WANTED TO TALK TO ME ABOUT, I THINK.
BZZ BZZ
I HAVE TO TAKE THIS CALL. ALL I CAN SAY IS THEY WERE BOTH ALIVE WHEN I LEFT THEM BACKSTAGE.
BZZZ BZZ
SEE YOU BACK AT THE SUMMIT.
BOTH? WHAT DO YOU MEAN BOTH? WHO WAS WITH DARIAN?
WE'RE WATCHING YOU, WILEY.

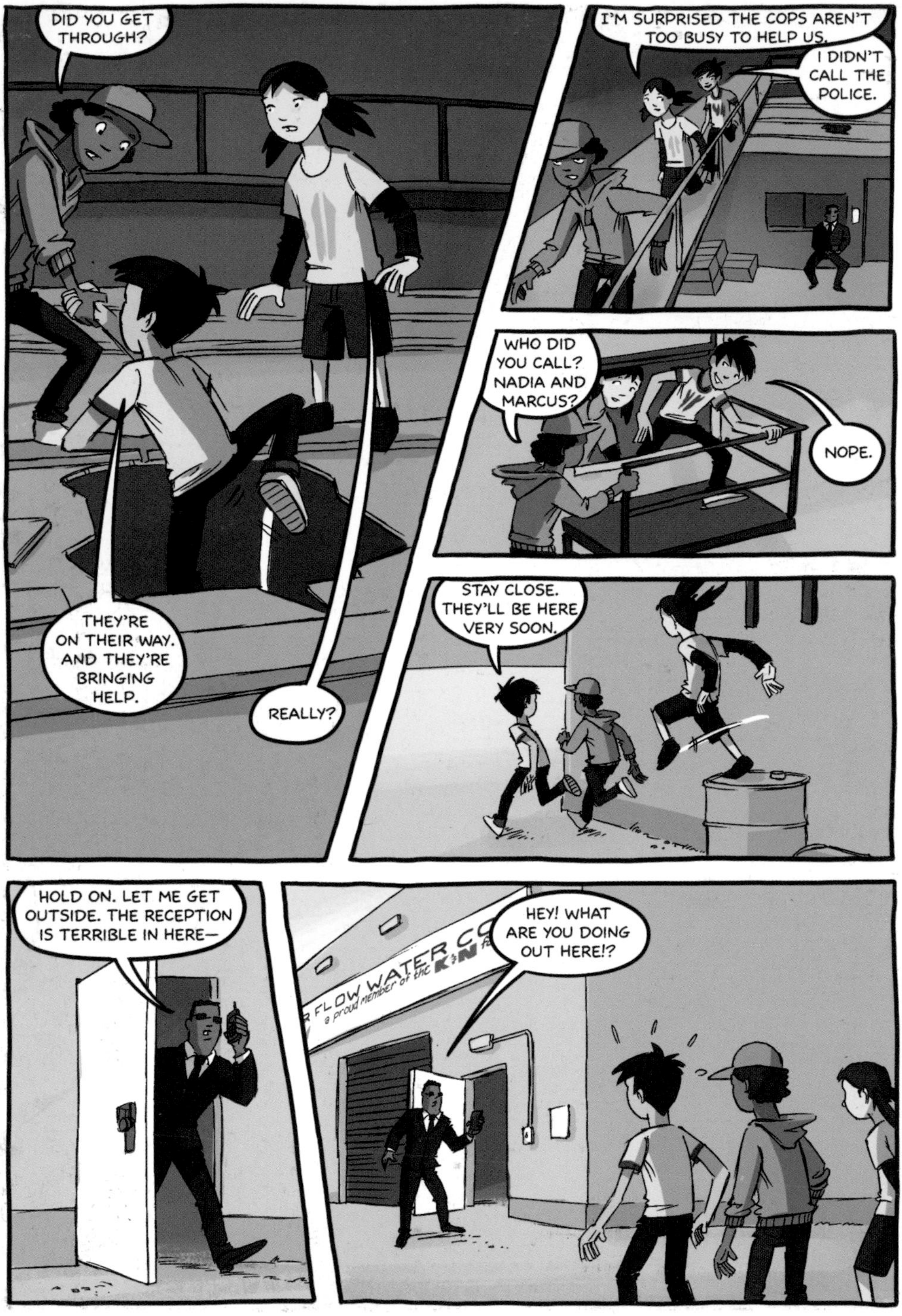
DID YOU GET THROUGH?
THEY'RE ON THEIR WAY. AND THEY'RE BRINGING HELP.
REALLY?
I'M SURPRISED THE COPS AREN'T TOO BUSY TO HELP US.
I DIDN'T CALL THE POLICE.
WHO DID YOU CALL? NADIA AND MARCUS?
NOPE.
STAY CLOSE. THEY'LL BE HERE VERY SOON.
HOLD ON. LET ME GET OUTSIDE. THE RECEPTION IS TERRIBLE IN HERE—
FLOW WATER CO
a proud member of the
HEY! WHAT ARE YOU DOING OUT HERE!?

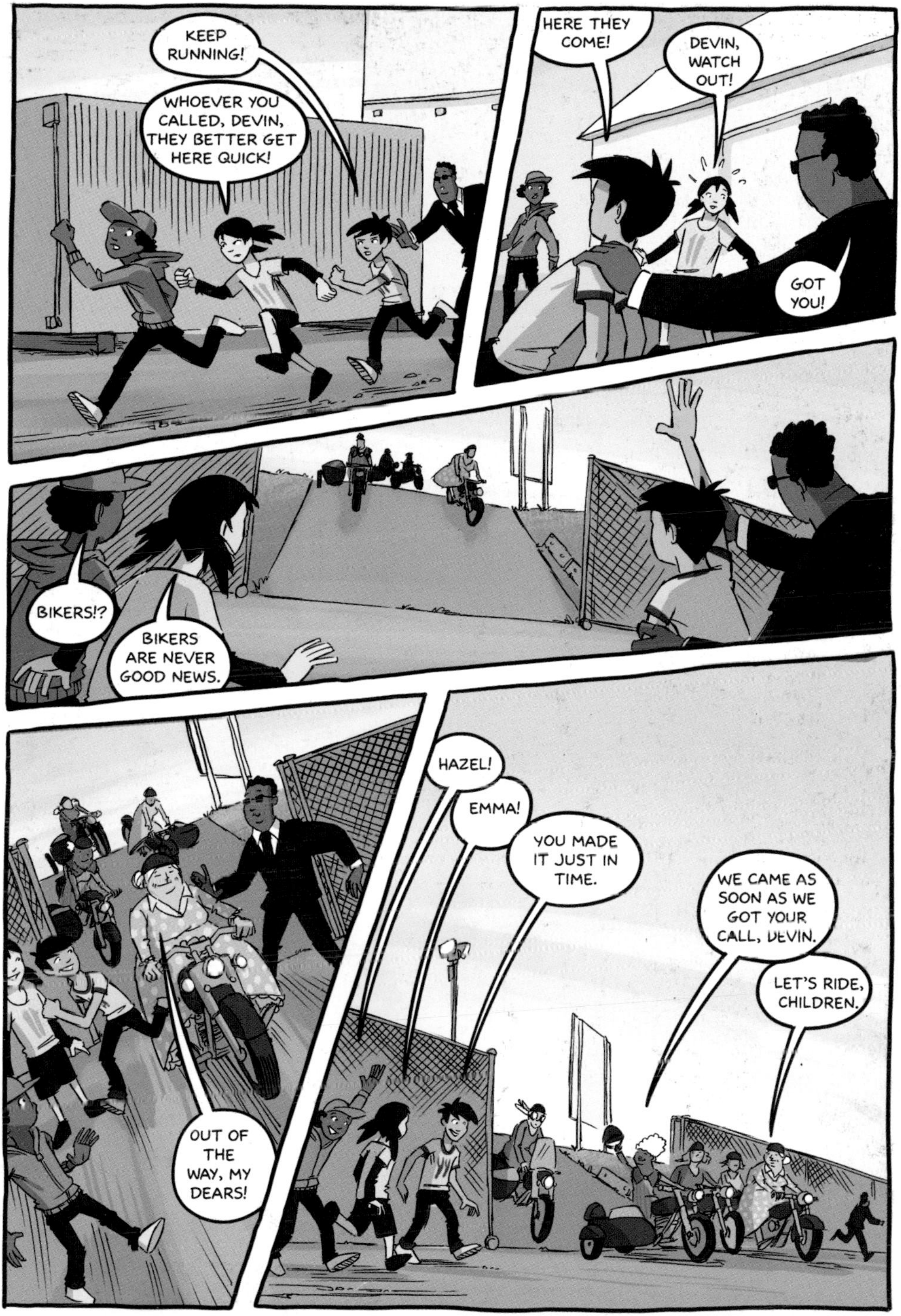
KEEP RUNNING!
WHOEVER YOU CALLED, DEVIN, THEY BETTER GET HERE QUICK!
HERE THEY COME!
DEVIN, WATCH OUT!
GOT YOU!
BIKERS!?
BIKERS ARE NEVER GOOD NEWS.
OUT OF THE WAY, MY DEARS!
HAZEL!
EMMA!
YOU MADE IT JUST IN TIME.
WE CAME AS SOON AS WE GOT YOUR CALL, DEVIN.
LET'S RIDE, CHILDREN.

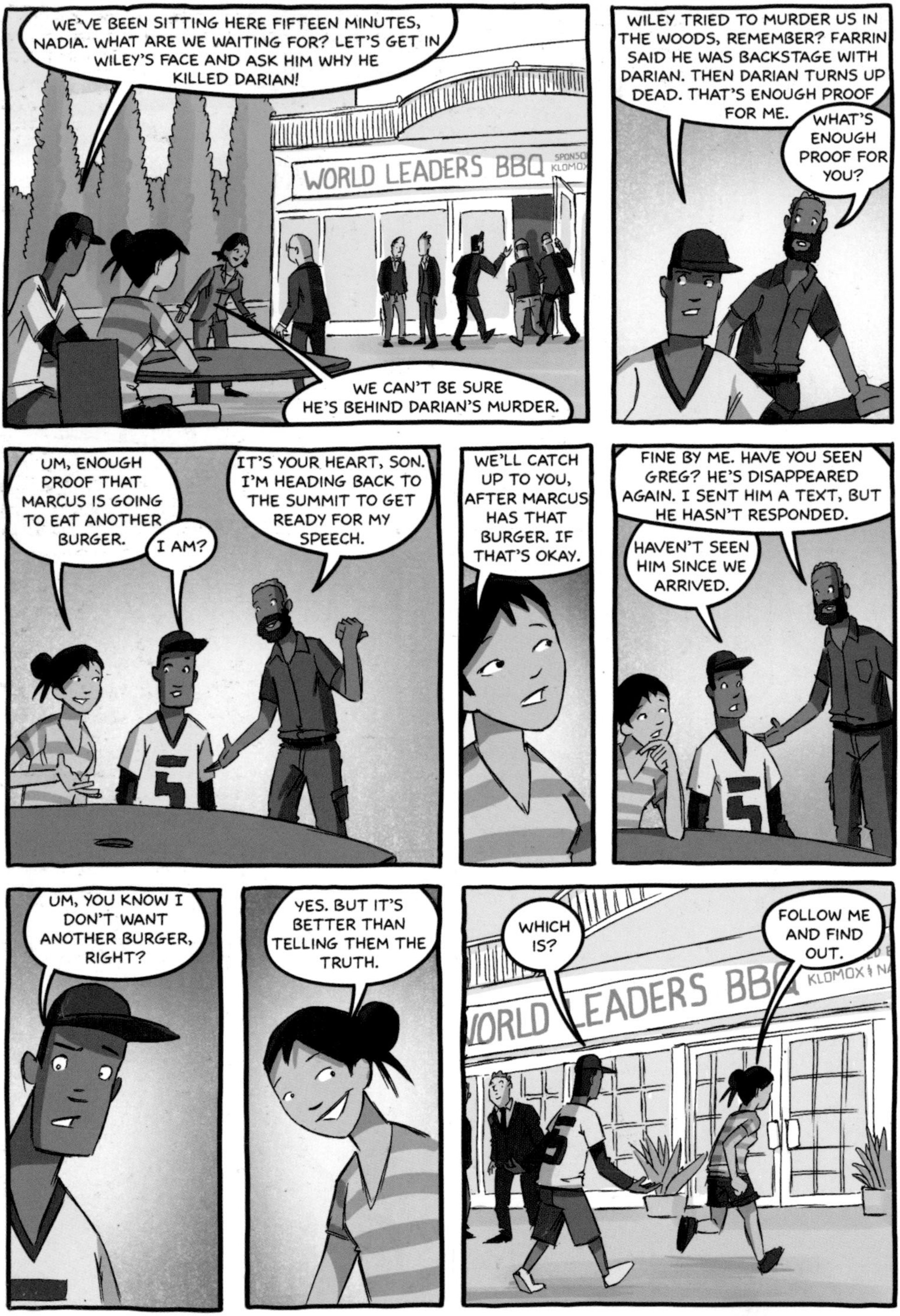
WE'VE BEEN SITTING HERE FIFTEEN MINUTES, NADIA. WHAT ARE WE WAITING FOR? LET'S GET IN WILEY'S FACE AND ASK HIM WHY HE KILLED DARIAN!
WORLD LEADERS BBQ
SPONSO
KLOMOX
WE CAN'T BE SURE HE'S BEHIND DARIAN'S MURDER.
WILEY TRIED TO MURDER US IN THE WOODS, REMEMBER? FARRIN SAID HE WAS BACKSTAGE WITH DARIAN. THEN DARIAN TURNS UP DEAD. THAT'S ENOUGH PROOF FOR ME.
WHAT'S ENOUGH PROOF FOR YOU?
UM, ENOUGH PROOF THAT MARCUS IS GOING TO EAT ANOTHER BURGER.
I AM?
IT'S YOUR HEART, SON. I'M HEADING BACK TO THE SUMMIT TO GET READY FOR MY SPEECH.
WE'LL CATCH UP TO YOU, AFTER MARCUS HAS THAT BURGER. IF THAT'S OKAY.
FINE BY ME. HAVE YOU SEEN GREG? HE'S DISAPPEARED AGAIN. I SENT HIM A TEXT, BUT HE HASN'T RESPONDED.
HAVEN'T SEEN HIM SINCE WE ARRIVED.
UM, YOU KNOW I DON'T WANT ANOTHER BURGER, RIGHT?
YES. BUT IT'S BETTER THAN TELLING THEM THE TRUTH.
WHICH IS?
FOLLOW ME AND FIND OUT.
WORLD LEADERS BBQ
KLOMOX

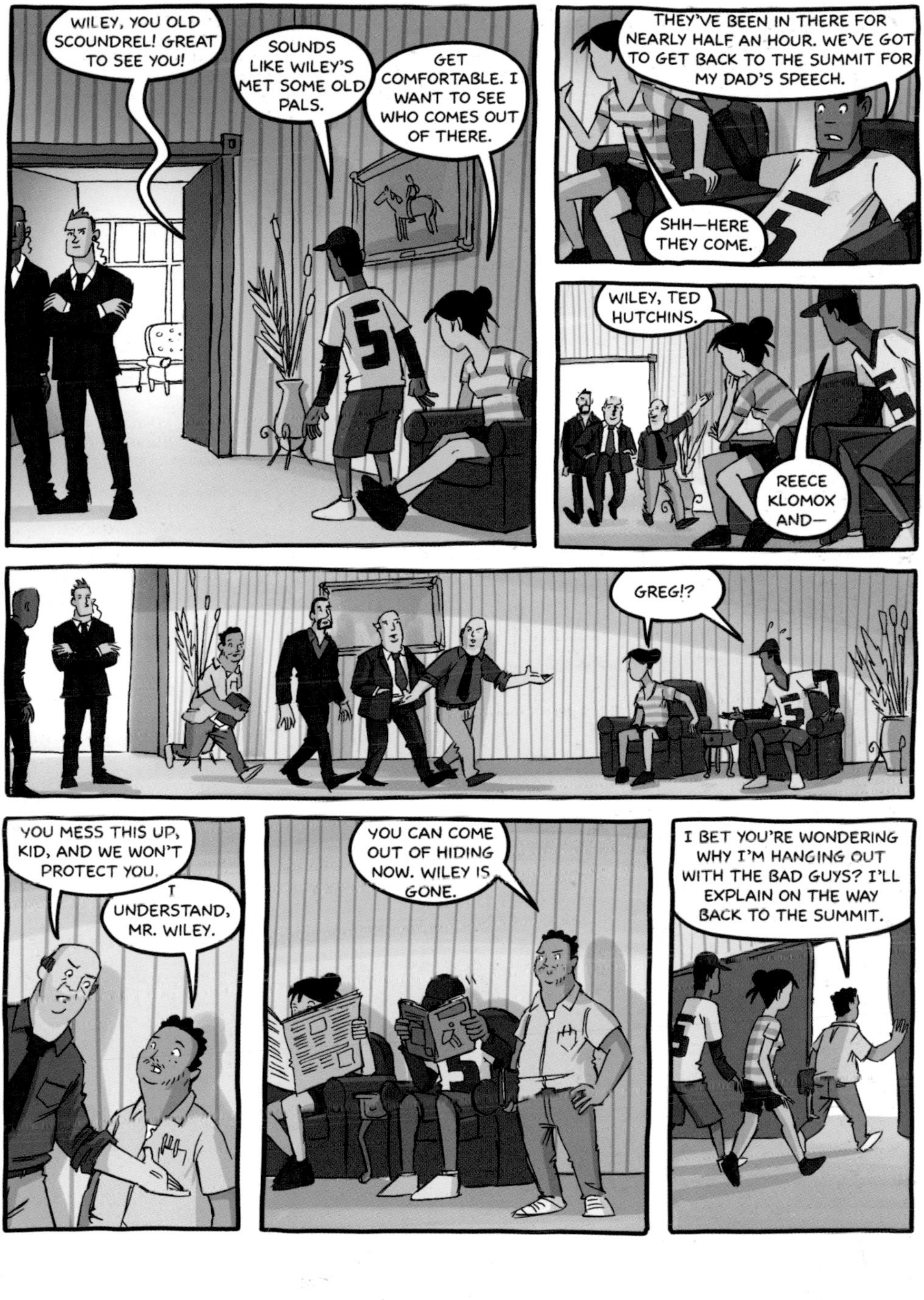

WILEY, YOU OLD SCOUNDREL! GREAT TO SEE YOU!
SOUNDS LIKE WILEY'S MET SOME OLD PALS.
GET COMFORTABLE. I WANT TO SEE WHO COMES OUT OF THERE.
THEY'VE BEEN IN THERE FOR NEARLY HALF AN HOUR. WE'VE GOT TO GET BACK TO THE SUMMIT FOR MY DAD'S SPEECH.
SHH—HERE THEY COME.
WILEY, TED HUTCHINS.
REECE KLOMOX AND—
GREG!?
YOU MESS THIS UP, KID, AND WE WON'T PROTECT YOU.
I UNDERSTAND, MR. WILEY.
YOU CAN COME OUT OF HIDING NOW. WILEY IS GONE.
I BET YOU'RE WONDERING WHY I'M HANGING OUT WITH THE BAD GUYS? I'LL EXPLAIN ON THE WAY BACK TO THE SUMMIT.

CHAPTER 6
WATER WAR

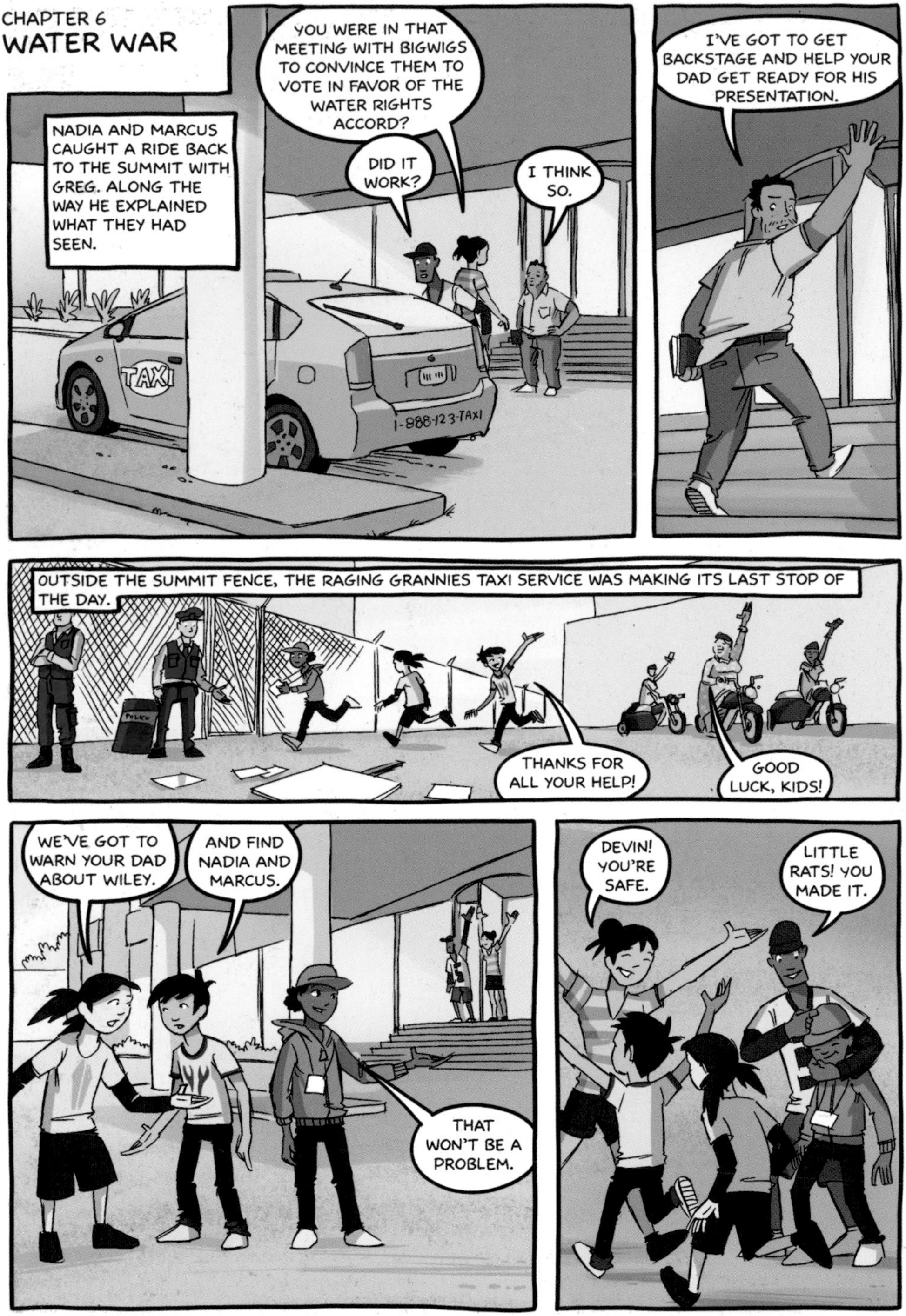
NADIA AND MARCUS CAUGHT A RIDE BACK TO THE SUMMIT WITH GREG. ALONG THE WAY HE EXPLAINED WHAT THEY HAD SEEN.
YOU WERE IN THAT MEETING WITH BIGWIGS TO CONVINCE THEM TO VOTE IN FAVOR OF THE WATER RIGHTS ACCORD?
DID IT WORK?
I THINK SO.
TAXI
1-888-123-TAXI
I'VE GOT TO GET BACKSTAGE AND HELP YOUR DAD GET READY FOR HIS PRESENTATION.
OUTSIDE THE SUMMIT FENCE, THE RAGING GRANNIES TAXI SERVICE WAS MAKING ITS LAST STOP OF THE DAY.
THANKS FOR ALL YOUR HELP!
GOOD LUCK, KIDS!
WE'VE GOT TO WARN YOUR DAD ABOUT WILEY.
AND FIND NADIA AND MARCUS.
THAT WON'T BE A PROBLEM.
DEVIN! YOU'RE SAFE.
LITTLE RATS! YOU MADE IT.

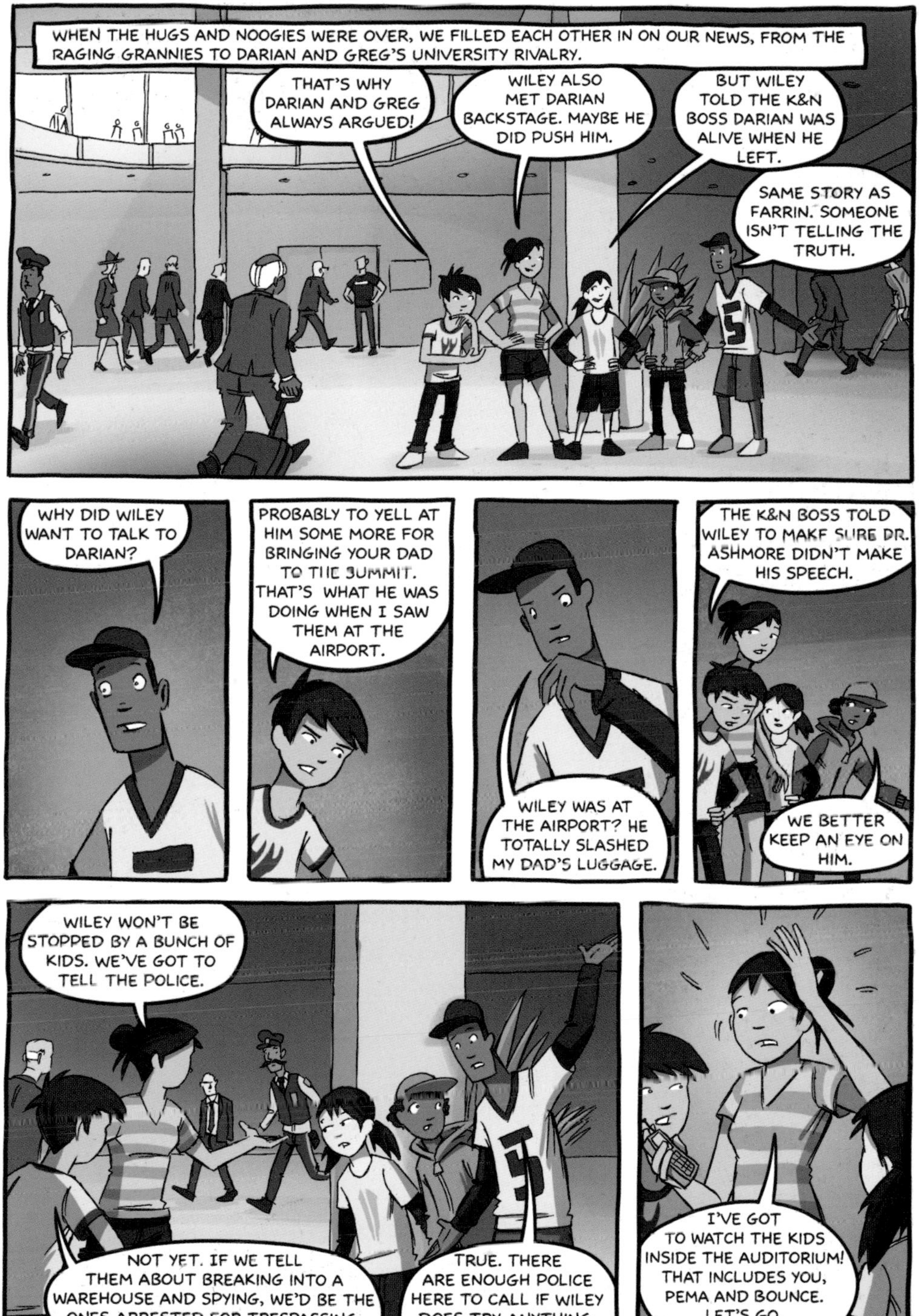
WHEN THE HUGS AND NOOGIES WERE OVER, WE FILLED EACH OTHER IN ON OUR NEWS, FROM THE RAGING GRANNIES TO DARIAN AND GREG'S UNIVERSITY RIVALRY.
THAT'S WHY DARIAN AND GREG ALWAYS ARGUED!
WILEY ALSO MET DARIAN BACKSTAGE. MAYBE HE DID PUSH HIM.
BUT WILEY TOLD THE K&N BOSS DARIAN WAS ALIVE WHEN HE LEFT.
SAME STORY AS FARRIN. SOMEONE ISN'T TELLING THE TRUTH.
WHY DID WILEY WANT TO TALK TO DARIAN?
PROBABLY TO YELL AT HIM SOME MORE FOR BRINGING YOUR DAD TO THE SUMMIT. THAT'S WHAT HE WAS DOING WHEN I SAW THEM AT THE AIRPORT.
WILEY WAS AT THE AIRPORT? HE TOTALLY SLASHED MY DAD'S LUGGAGE.
THE K&N BOSS TOLD WILEY TO MAKE SURE DR. ASHMORE DIDN'T MAKE HIS SPEECH.
WE BETTER KEEP AN EYE ON HIM.
WILEY WON'T BE STOPPED BY A BUNCH OF KIDS. WE'VE GOT TO TELL THE POLICE.
NOT YET. IF WE TELL THEM ABOUT BREAKING INTO A WAREHOUSE AND SPYING, WE'D BE THE ONES ARRESTED FOR TRESPASSING.
TRUE. THERE ARE ENOUGH POLICE HERE TO CALL IF WILEY DOES TRY ANYTHING.
I'VE GOT TO WATCH THE KIDS INSIDE THE AUDITORIUM! THAT INCLUDES YOU, PEMA AND BOUNCE. LET'S GO.

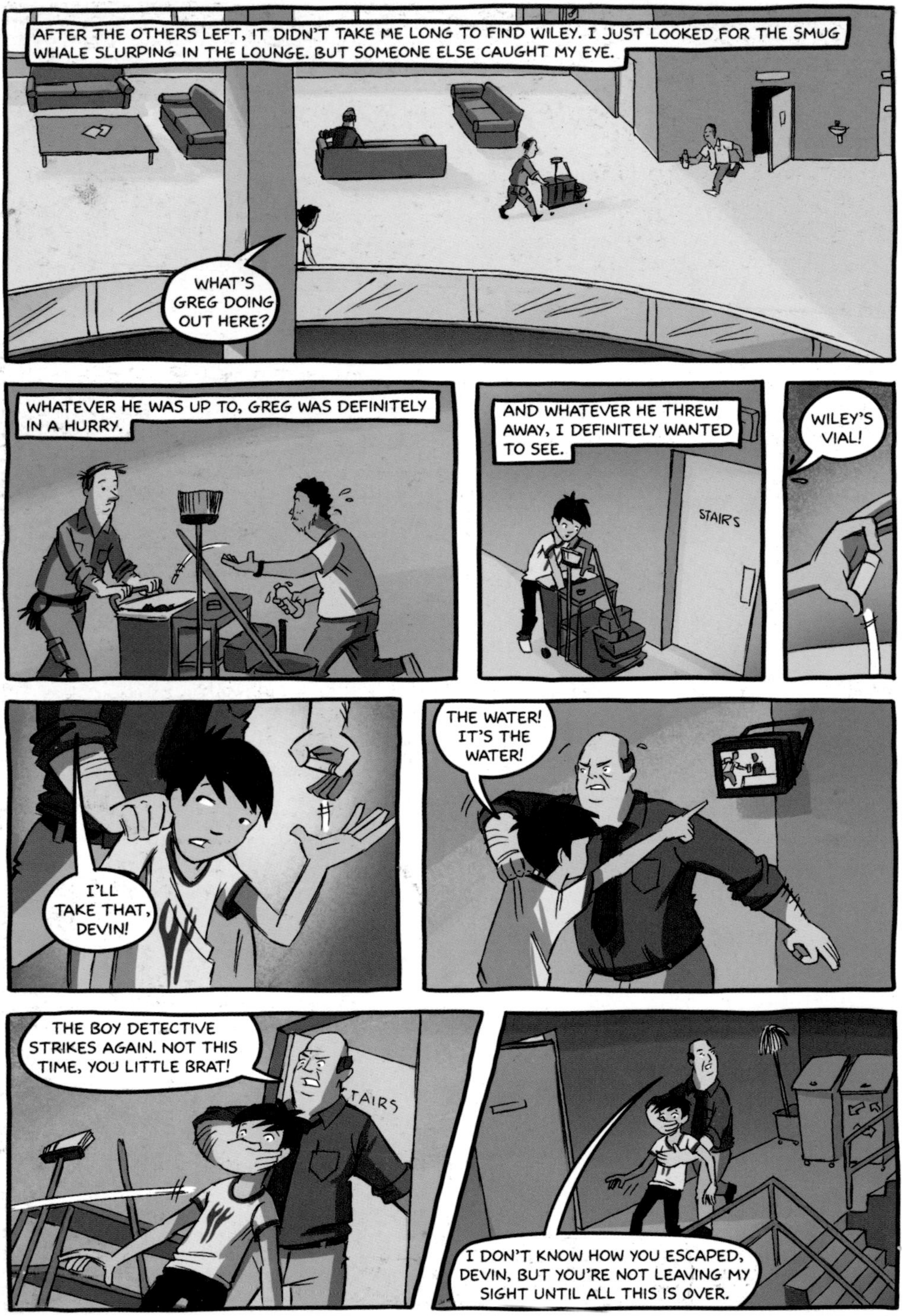
AFTER THE OTHERS LEFT, IT DIDN'T TAKE ME LONG TO FIND WILEY. I JUST LOOKED FOR THE SMUG WHALE SLURPING IN THE LOUNGE. BUT SOMEONE ELSE CAUGHT MY EYE.
WHAT'S GREG DOING OUT HERE?
WHATEVER HE WAS UP TO, GREG WAS DEFINITELY IN A HURRY.
AND WHATEVER HE THREW AWAY, I DEFINITELY WANTED TO SEE.
STAIR'S
WILEY'S VIAL!
I'LL TAKE THAT, DEVIN!
THE WATER! IT'S THE WATER!
THE BOY DETECTIVE STRIKES AGAIN. NOT THIS TIME, YOU LITTLE BRAT!
STAIRS
I DON'T KNOW HOW YOU ESCAPED, DEVIN, BUT YOU'RE NOT LEAVING MY SIGHT UNTIL ALL THIS IS OVER.

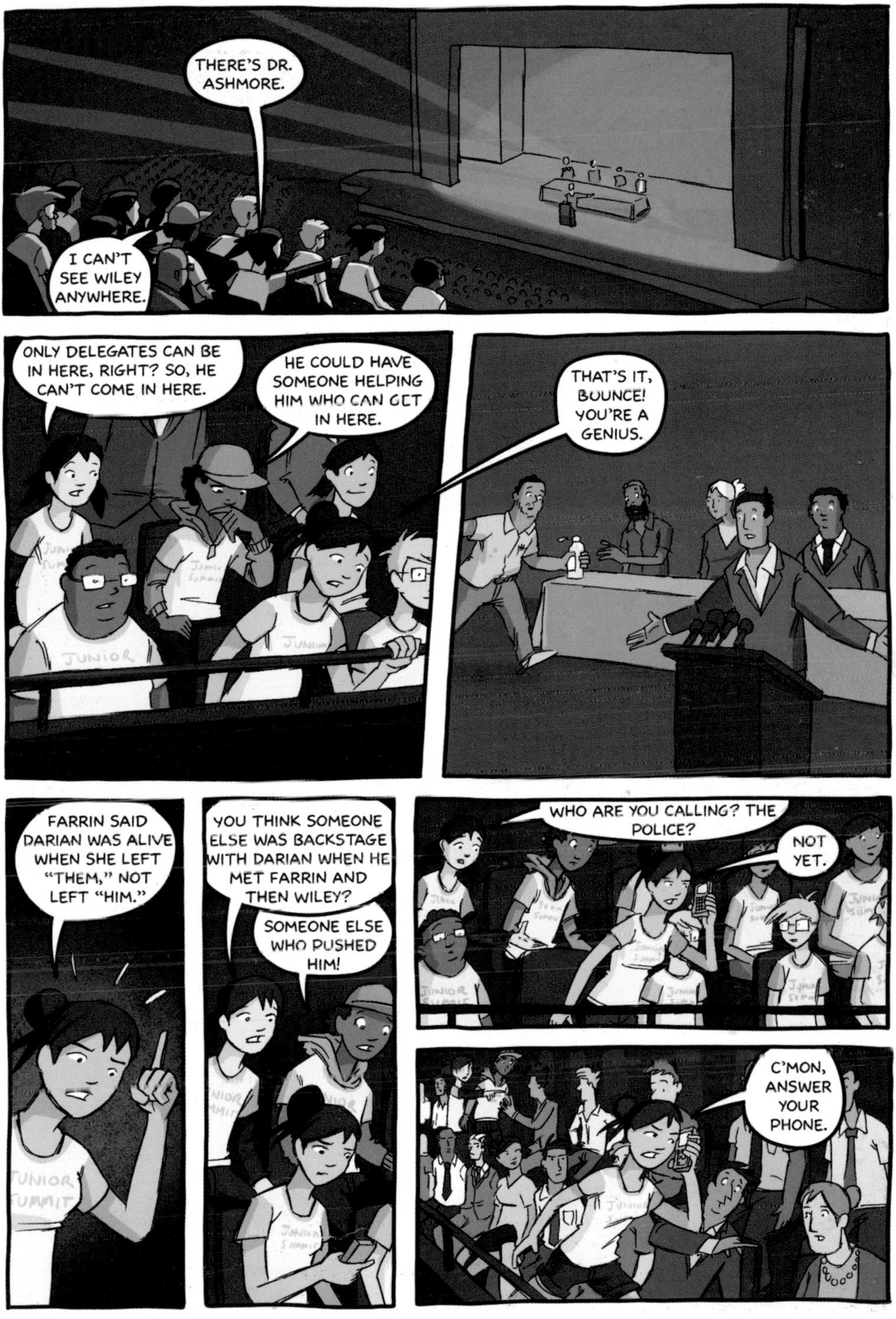
THERE'S DR. ASHMORE.
I CAN'T SEE WILEY ANYWHERE.
ONLY DELEGATES CAN BE IN HERE, RIGHT? SO, HE CAN'T COME IN HERE.
HE COULD HAVE SOMEONE HELPING HIM WHO CAN GET IN HERE.
THAT'S IT, BOUNCE! YOU'RE A GENIUS.
FARRIN SAID DARIAN WAS ALIVE WHEN SHE LEFT "THEM," NOT LEFT "HIM."
YOU THINK SOMEONE ELSE WAS BACKSTAGE WITH DARIAN WHEN HE MET FARRIN AND THEN WILEY?
SOMEONE ELSE WHO PUSHED HIM!
WHO ARE YOU CALLING? THE POLICE?
NOT YET.
C'MON, ANSWER YOUR PHONE.

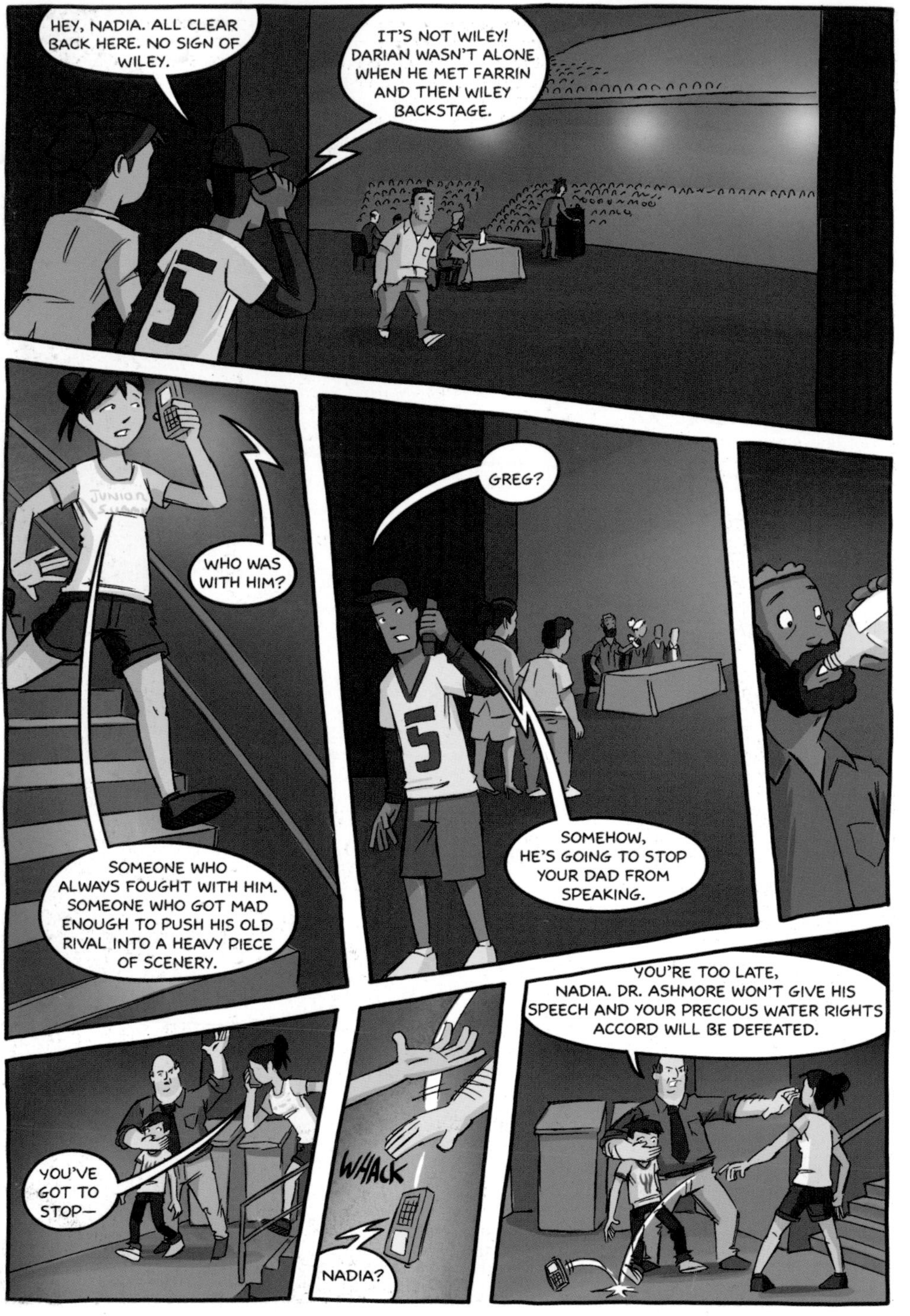
HEY, NADIA. ALL CLEAR BACK HERE. NO SIGN OF WILEY.
IT'S NOT WILEY! DARIAN WASN'T ALONE WHEN HE MET FARRIN AND THEN WILEY BACKSTAGE.
WHO WAS WITH HIM?
SOMEONE WHO ALWAYS FOUGHT WITH HIM. SOMEONE WHO GOT MAD ENOUGH TO PUSH HIS OLD RIVAL INTO A HEAVY PIECE OF SCENERY.
GREG?
SOMEHOW, HE'S GOING TO STOP YOUR DAD FROM SPEAKING.
YOU'VE GOT TO STOP—
WHACK
NADIA?
YOU'RE TOO LATE, NADIA. DR. ASHMORE WON'T GIVE HIS SPEECH AND YOUR PRECIOUS WATER RIGHTS ACCORD WILL BE DEFEATED.

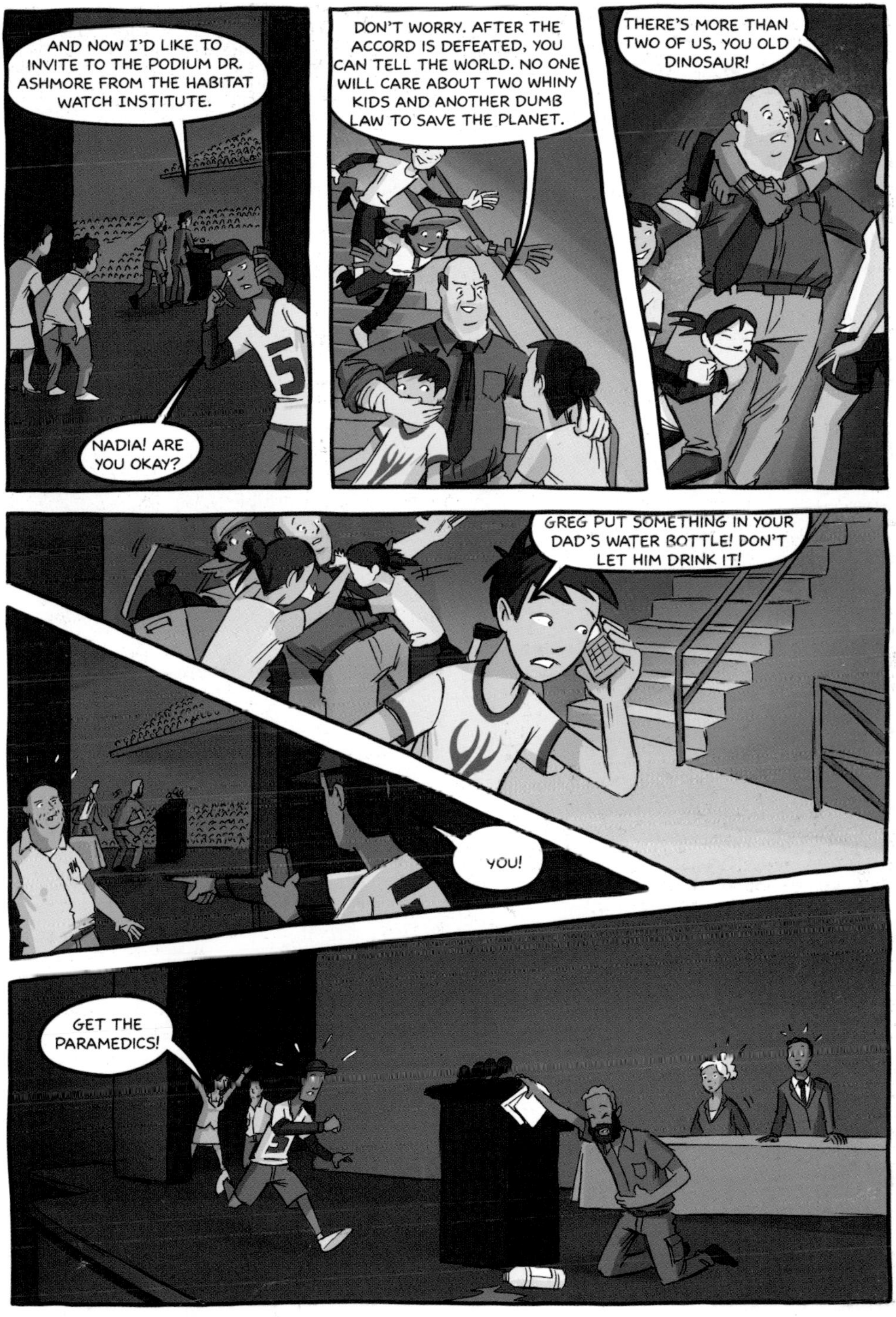
AND NOW I'D LIKE TO INVITE TO THE PODIUM DR. ASHMORE FROM THE HABITAT WATCH INSTITUTE.
NADIA! ARE YOU OKAY?
DON'T WORRY. AFTER THE ACCORD IS DEFEATED, YOU CAN TELL THE WORLD. NO ONE WILL CARE ABOUT TWO WHINY KIDS AND ANOTHER DUMB LAW TO SAVE THE PLANET.
THERE'S MORE THAN TWO OF US, YOU OLD DINOSAUR!
GREG PUT SOMETHING IN YOUR DAD'S WATER BOTTLE! DON'T LET HIM DRINK IT!
YOU!
GET THE PARAMEDICS!

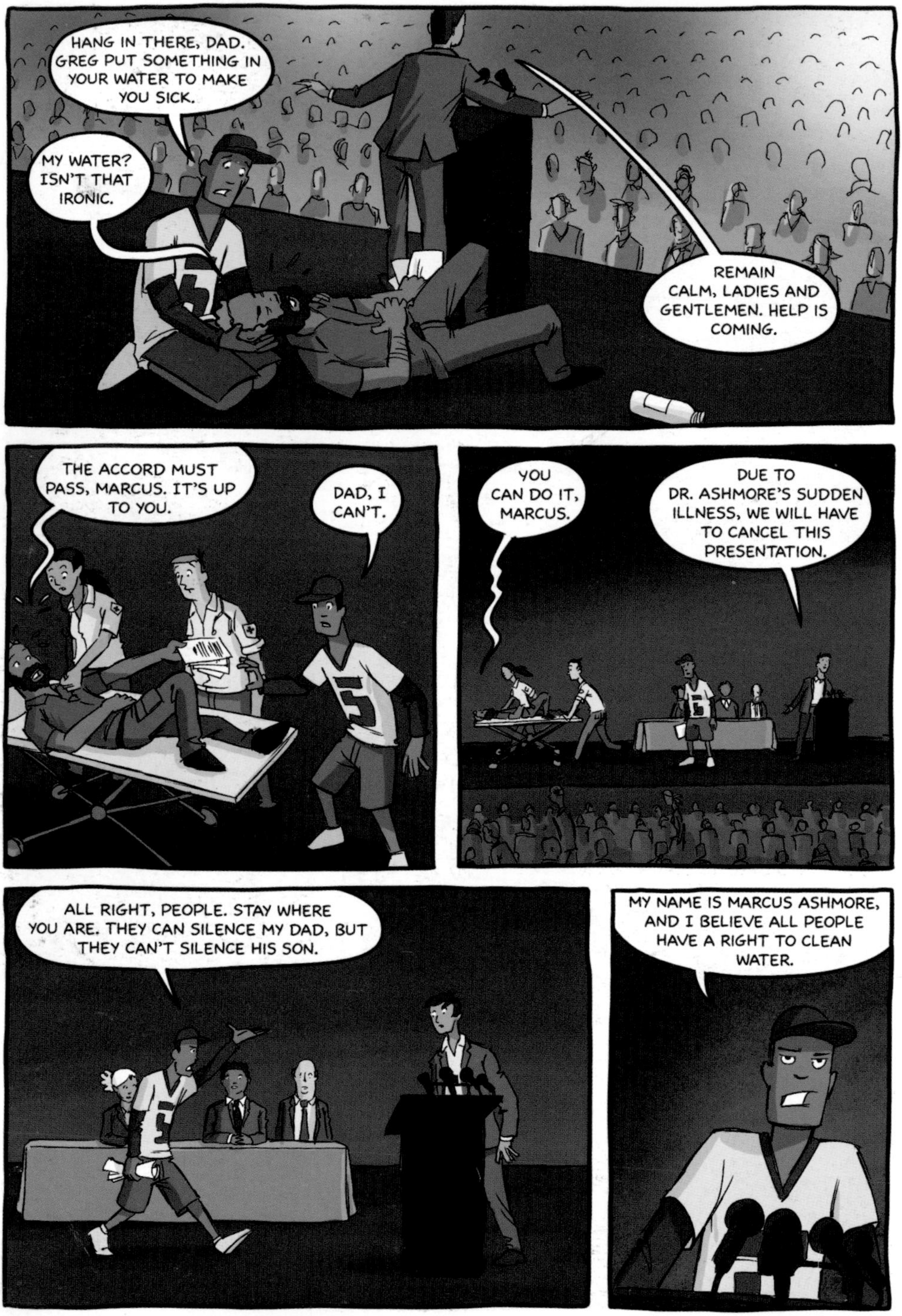
HANG IN THERE, DAD. GREG PUT SOMETHING IN YOUR WATER TO MAKE YOU SICK.
MY WATER? ISN'T THAT IRONIC.
REMAIN CALM, LADIES AND GENTLEMEN. HELP IS COMING.
THE ACCORD MUST PASS, MARCUS. IT'S UP TO YOU.
DAD, I CAN'T.
YOU CAN DO IT, MARCUS.
DUE TO DR. ASHMORE'S SUDDEN ILLNESS, WE WILL HAVE TO CANCEL THIS PRESENTATION.
ALL RIGHT, PEOPLE. STAY WHERE YOU ARE. THEY CAN SILENCE MY DAD, BUT THEY CAN'T SILENCE HIS SON.
MY NAME IS MARCUS ASHMORE, AND I BELIEVE ALL PEOPLE HAVE A RIGHT TO CLEAN WATER.

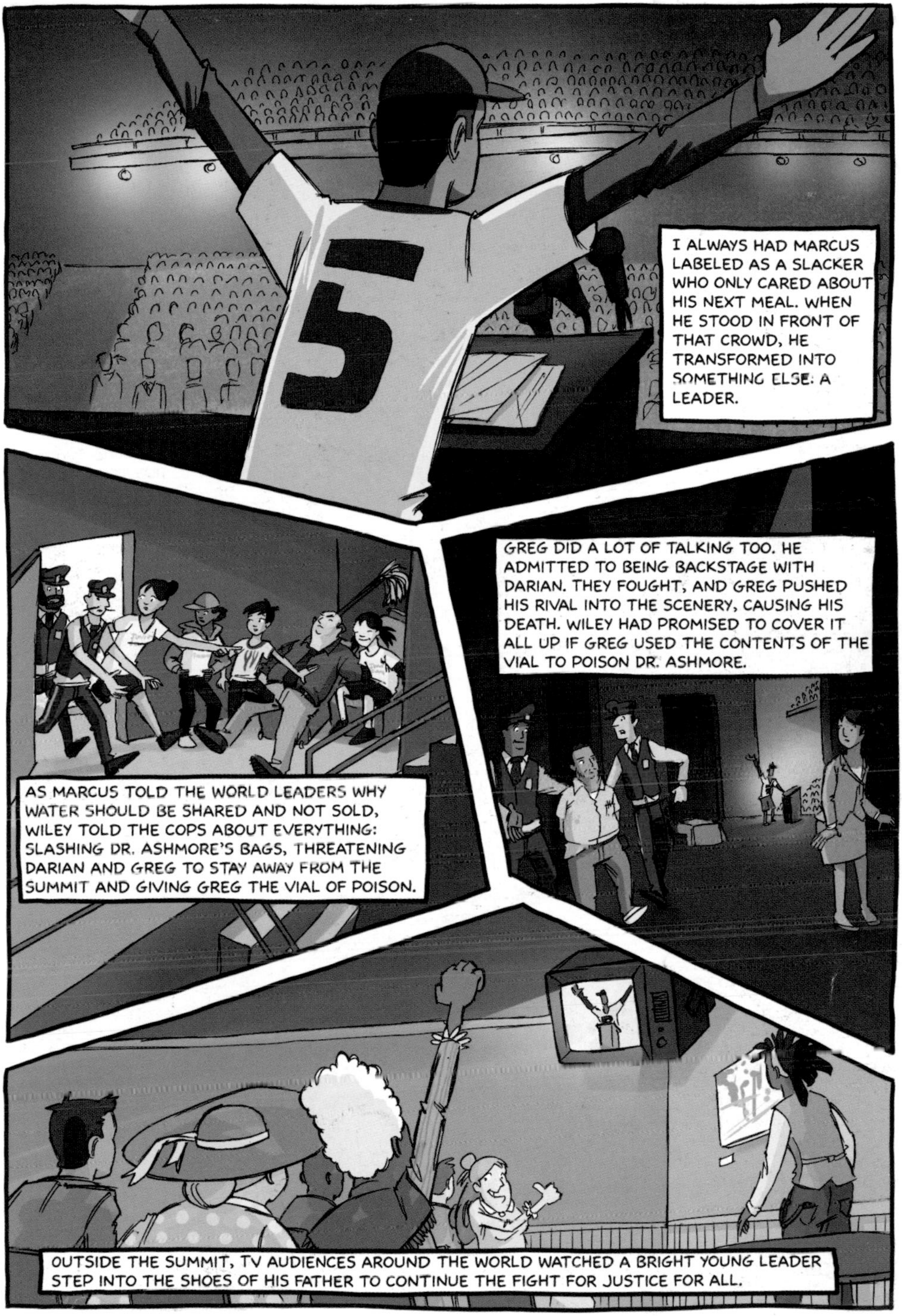
I ALWAYS HAD MARCUS LABELED AS A SLACKER WHO ONLY CARED ABOUT HIS NEXT MEAL. WHEN HE STOOD IN FRONT OF THAT CROWD, HE TRANSFORMED INTO SOMETHING ELSE: A LEADER.
AS MARCUS TOLD THE WORLD LEADERS WHY WATER SHOULD BE SHARED AND NOT SOLD, WILEY TOLD THE COPS ABOUT EVERYTHING: SLASHING DR. ASHMORE'S BAGS, THREATENING DARIAN AND GREG TO STAY AWAY FROM THE SUMMIT AND GIVING GREG THE VIAL OF POISON.
GREG DID A LOT OF TALKING TOO. HE ADMITTED TO BEING BACKSTAGE WITH DARIAN. THEY FOUGHT, AND GREG PUSHED HIS RIVAL INTO THE SCENERY, CAUSING HIS DEATH. WILEY HAD PROMISED TO COVER IT ALL UP IF GREG USED THE CONTENTS OF THE VIAL TO POISON DR. ASHMORE.
OUTSIDE THE SUMMIT, TV AUDIENCES AROUND THE WORLD WATCHED A BRIGHT YOUNG LEADER STEP INTO THE SHOES OF HIS FATHER TO CONTINUE THE FIGHT FOR JUSTICE FOR ALL.

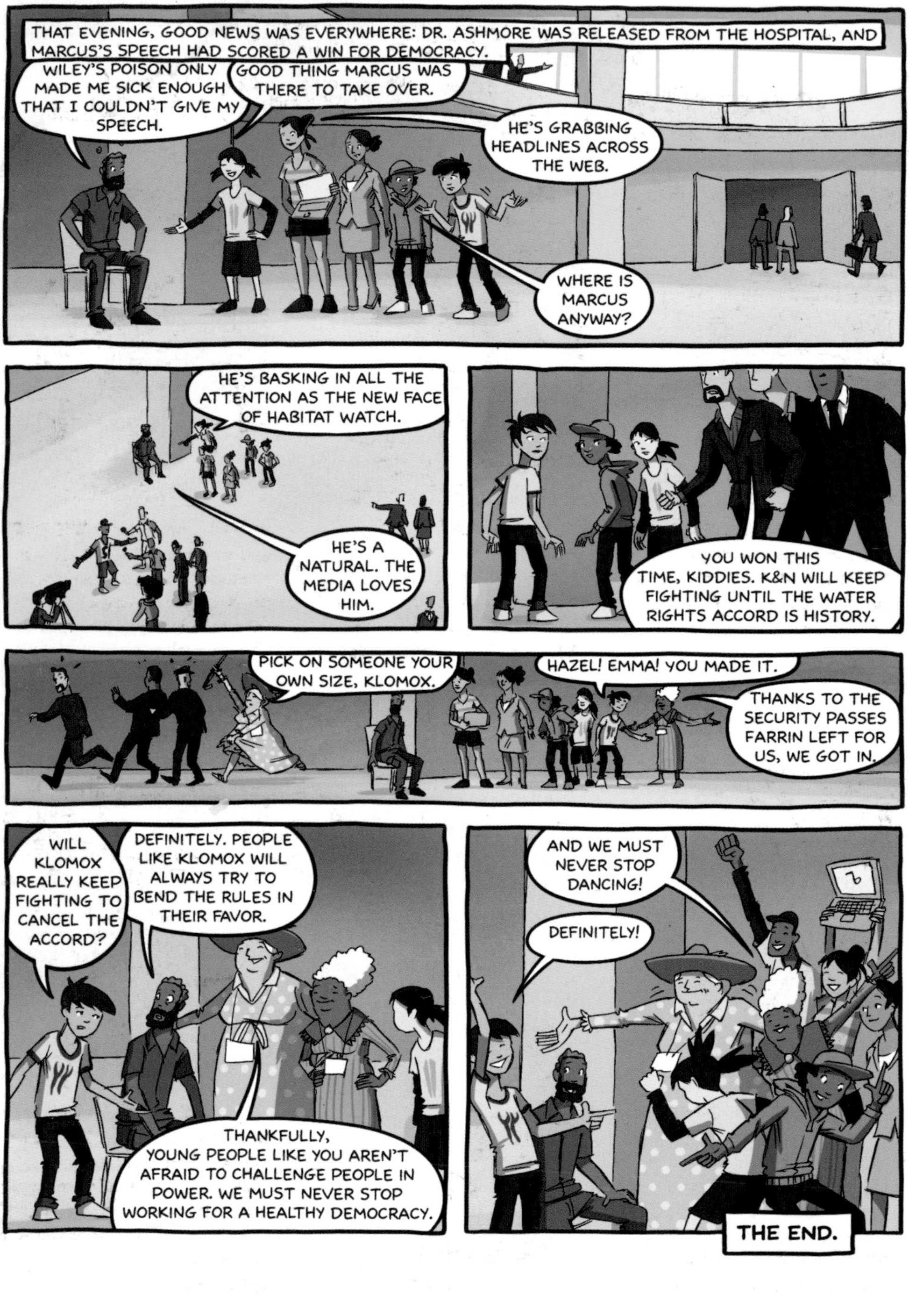
THAT EVENING, GOOD NEWS WAS EVERYWHERE: DR. ASHMORE WAS RELEASED FROM THE HOSPITAL, AND MARCUS'S SPEECH HAD SCORED A WIN FOR DEMOCRACY.
WILEY'S POISON ONLY MADE ME SICK ENOUGH THAT I COULDN'T GIVE MY SPEECH.
GOOD THING MARCUS WAS THERE TO TAKE OVER.
HE'S GRABBING HEADLINES ACROSS THE WEB.
WHERE IS MARCUS ANYWAY?
HE'S BASKING IN ALL THE ATTENTION AS THE NEW FACE OF HABITAT WATCH.
HE'S A NATURAL. THE MEDIA LOVES HIM.
YOU WON THIS TIME, KIDDIES. K&N WILL KEEP FIGHTING UNTIL THE WATER RIGHTS ACCORD IS HISTORY.
PICK ON SOMEONE YOUR OWN SIZE, KLOMOX.
HAZEL! EMMA! YOU MADE IT.
THANKS TO THE SECURITY PASSES FARRIN LEFT FOR US, WE GOT IN.
WILL KLOMOX REALLY KEEP FIGHTING TO CANCEL THE ACCORD?
DEFINITELY. PEOPLE LIKE KLOMOX WILL ALWAYS TRY TO BEND THE RULES IN THEIR FAVOR.
THANKFULLY, YOUNG PEOPLE LIKE YOU AREN'T AFRAID TO CHALLENGE PEOPLE IN POWER. WE MUST NEVER STOP WORKING FOR A HEALTHY DEMOCRACY.
AND WE MUST NEVER STOP DANCING!
DEFINITELY!
THE END.

GRAB THESE OTHER GRAPHIC GUIDE ADVENTURES...

WILD RIDE
A GRAPHIC GUIDE ADVENTURE
LIAM O'DONNELL
MIKE DEAS

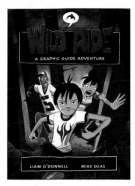

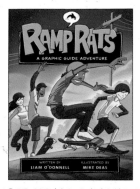

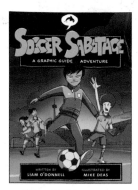

AFTER THEIR PLANE GOES down in rugged wilderness, Devin, Nadia and Marcus struggle to survive. Adventure, danger and survival skills (and bears. Oh my!).

978-1-55143-756-9

RAMP RATS
A GRAPHIC GUIDE ADVENTURE
WRITTEN BY
LIAM O'DONNELL
ILLUSTRATED BY
MIKE DEAS

BETWEEN LEARNING HOW to ollie and do a 50-50 grind, Bounce and his friends have to avoid the skate-park goons and take on a gang of outlaw bikers. A Junior Library Guild selection.

978-1-55143-880-1

SOCCER SABOTAGE
A GRAPHIC GUIDE ADVENTURE
WRITTEN BY
LIAM O'DONNELL
ILLUSTRATED BY
MIKE DEAS

WITH SUSPICIOUS ACCIDENTS and mounting threats against the team, it's up to Devin and his sister Nadia to pull the team together and take a run at the championship.

978-1-55143-884-9

MEDIA MELTDOWN
A GRAPHIC GUIDE ADVENTURE
WRITTEN BY
LIAM O'DONNELL
ILLUSTRATED BY
MIKE DEAS

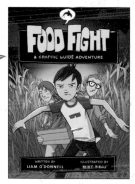

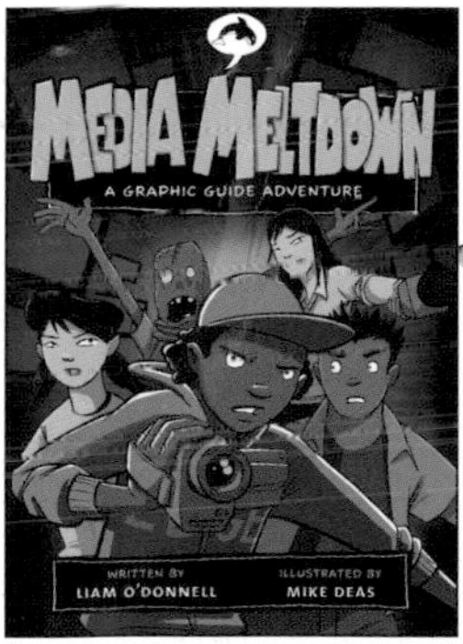

WHEN A DEVELOPER TRIES to force the sale of a local farm, Pema, Bounce and Jagroop decide to expose him through the media. Some frightening lessons about media consolidation and the power of money over truth.

978-1-55469-065-7

CHECK OUT
WWW.MEDIAMELTDOWN.NET
AND WWW.FOOD-FIGHT.NET
FOR INFORMATION,
GAMES AND MORE!

FOOD FIGHT
A GRAPHIC GUIDE ADVENTURE
WRITTEN BY
LIAM O'DONNELL
ILLUSTRATED BY

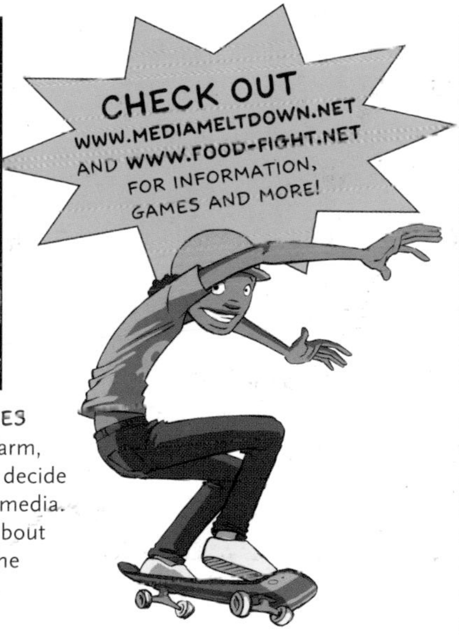

STUCK AT SUMMER CAMP while their mother works on an agricultural research project, Devin and Nadia stumbe upon a conspiracy involving genetically modified food and unscrupulous scientists.

978-1-55469-067-1

ABOUT THE AUTHOR

FROM CHAPTER BOOKS TO COMIC STRIPS, LIAM O'DONNELL WRITES FICTION AND NONFICTION FOR YOUNG READERS. HE IS THE AUTHOR OF THE AWARD-WINNING SERIES "MAX FINDER MYSTERY." LIAM LIVES IN TORONTO, ONTARIO. VISIT LIAM AT: LIAMODONNELL.COM

ABOUT THE ILLUSTRATOR

MIKE DEAS IS A TALENTED ILLUSTRATOR IN A NUMBER OF DIFFERENT GENRES. HE GRADUATED FROM CAPILANO COLLEGE'S COMMERCIAL ANIMATION PROGRAM AND HAS WORKED AS A GAME DEVELOPER. MIKE LIVES IN VICTORIA, BRITISH COLUMBIA.